ATALA

LECTOR HOUSE PUBLIC DOMAIN WORKS

ATALA

FRANÇOIS AUGUSTE DE CHATEAUBRIAND

ISBN: 978-93-5344-854-7

Published: -

© LECTOR HOUSE LLP

LECTOR HOUSE LLP
E-MAIL: lectorpublishing@gmail.com

ATALA

BY

FRANÇOIS AUGUSTE DE CHATEAUBRIAND

ILLUSTRATED
BY
GUSTAVE DORÉ

CONTENTS

LIST OF ILLUSTRATIONS

INTRODUCTION.

Among the illustrious names which adorn the annals of France, that of François Auguste de Chateaubriand, the author of "Atala," "Les Martyrs," "The Last of the Abencerages," and many other brilliant and renowned works, occupies a proud pre-eminence. But his fame rests not merely upon his literary achievements. His services as a statesman and the record and example of his private life-even his sufferings and misfortunes-have served to enhance his reputation and endear his memory, both among his own countrymen, and among just, noble and patriotic minds in other lands. He was great both by his character and abilities; and, while his celebrity is undiminished by the lapse of time, his works are still read and will long continue to be read and admired, even through all changes in the manners and sentiments of mankind. Fashions and modes in literature and art, as in society, come and go; new institutions arise, demanding new methods and modifying cherished customs; and men's thoughts enlarge and widen with improved conditions, as with the inevitable progress of the age. But the master mind ever asserts its power. He who has once truly stirred the human heart in its purest depths speaks not alone to his own generation, but appeals to all other hearts and belongs to all his race. His good gifts are the birthright of the world. The rank of Chateaubriand has been fixed by the united judgment of his associates and his successors; and since time has allayed the fierce passions which raged in France during his lifetime, his character is more and more deeply respected and admired. His sincerity of purpose and enlightened understanding, his grandeur and nobility of thought, his energy of action and loftiness of aim, preserve for him ever his exalted position, made brilliant by the fires of genius and perpetuated by the force of truth.

Chateaubriand was born at St. Malo in September, 1768, and died in Paris, after an active and most eventful career, on the fourth of July, 1848. The earlier portion of his life was passed in the quiet of his home at Combourg. At the termination of his collegiate training at Dole and Rennes, he entered the army, in which he soon gained promotion. At about the age of nineteen he was presented at court, became acquainted with the fashionable world, and was received and welcomed into the choicest literary circles of Paris, where he gained the friendship of La Harpe, Fontanes, Malesherbes, and others among the distinguished savants of that period. It was a troubled and stormy epoch in France. The social and political forces which culminated in the great Revolution were beginning to be seriously felt, and faction, turbulence and anarchy were already rife in Paris when Chateaubriand left his native shores for America, moved by a desire to discover the northwest passage, but also with an attendant purpose, long cherished, of observing the mode of life and studying the characteristics of the aborigines, for the purpose of embodying in his writings the impressions thus gained of man in a primitive condition.

From this period to the time of his death his life was a singular series of vicissitudes—at one time the brilliant and revered statesman, at another the voluntary abdicator of all his rights and honors; and even, at one bitter passage of his existence, living in an unwarmed London garret and obtaining a precarious livelihood by giving lessons in his native tongue and translating for the booksellers.

The utter upheaval of affairs in France brought the greatest distress upon himself, his family and his immediate friends, and, with the sensitive heart of genius, the blows which had fallen so keenly doubtless engendered the melancholy cast with which his writings are sometimes tinged. His first work, an idyllic poem, showed little of the genius so finely developed in after years; but his finest literary productions—"The Martyrs," "The Last of the Abencerages" and "The Genius of Christianity," to which "Atala" and "René" properly belong—remain a splendid monument to his powers and exhibit his earnest desire to be numbered among the benefactors and enlighteners of mankind.

The present work, "Atala," is the gathered fruit of his previous studies amid the wilds of America. It abounds in sparkling description, romantic incident and sentiments tender and heroic. It is pervaded by purity of tone and elevation of thought, qualities the more commendable and marked because produced in an age proverbially lax and frivolous.

The illustrations of M. Doré have given an additional value to this tale, so simple, so unsophisticated, yet blooming with all the wild luxuriance of nature. The artist has added his gifts to those of the poet; and those acquainted only with his ready and original powers as the delineator of farce and drollery, or of the exceptionally tragic and horrible, will find new cause for admiration in these quiet renderings of the primeval beauties of the American wild—its plains and forests, its still lagoons and roaring cataracts, its mountain slopes and deep defiles—all its aspects of rudest workmanship—and will welcome these efforts of his genius in the lovely realm of descriptive art, wedded as they are to the exquisite simplicity of this Indian romance. As in his other works, here may be noted the same surpassing fertility of resource, the same alertness of intellect and readiness and swiftness of touch; but there may also be found new proofs of his complete sympathy with all that is picturesque in forest beauty and his high intuitive perception of every possible phase of nature in her wildest caprice and most tender bloom.

We append the following extracts from different prefaces to the author's writings, as constituting what is explanatory of the story that follows:

[From the Preface to the First Edition.]

"I was still very young when I conceived the idea of composing an epic on 'The Man of Nature,' to depict the manners of savages, by uniting them with some well-known event. After the discovery of America, I saw no subject more interesting, especially to Frenchmen, than the massacre of the Natchez colony in Louisiana, in 1727. All the Indian tribes conspiring, after two centuries of oppression, for the restoration of liberty to the New World, appeared to me to offer a subject almost as attractive as the conquest of Mexico. I put some fragments of the work to paper; but I soon found that I was weak in local coloring, and that, if I wished to produce a picture of real resemblance, it became necessary for me, in imitation of Homer's example, to visit the tribes I was desirous of describing.

"In 1789 I made M. de Malesherbes acquainted with my idea of going to America; but, wishing at the same time to give a useful object to my voyage, I formed the project of discovering the overland passage so long sought after, and concerning which even Captain Cook himself had left some doubts. I started, visited the American solitudes, and returned with plans for a second voyage, which was to last nine years. I proposed to traverse the entire continent of North America, afterwards to explore the coasts to the north of California, and to return by Hudson's Bay, rounding the pole. M. de Malesherbes undertook to submit my plans to the Government, and it was then that he listened to the first fragments of the little work I now offer to the public. The Revolution put a stop to all my projects. Covered with the blood of my only brother, of my sister-in-law, and of the illustrious old man, their father; having seen my mother and another talented sister die in consequence of the treatment they had undergone in prison, I wandered forth to foreign lands, where the only friend I had preserved stabbed himself in my arms.

"Of all my manuscripts upon America, I have only saved some fragments, 'Atala' in particular, which was itself but an episode of 'The Natchez.' 'Atala' was written in the desert, beneath the huts of the savages. I do not know whether the public will like the story, which quits all beaten tracks, and represents a nature and manners altogether foreign to Europe. There is no adventure in 'Atala.' It is a sort of poem, half descriptive, half dramatic. It consists entirely in the portraiture of two lovers walking and talking together in the solitudes, and in the picture of the trials of love in the midst of the calm of the desert. I have endeavored to give to this work the most antique forms. It is divided into Prologue, Recital and Epilogue. The principal parts of the story have each a denomination, such as 'The Hunters,' 'The Laborers,' etc.; and it was thus that, in the early ages of Greece, the rhapsodists sang, under different titles, fragments of the 'Iliad' and 'Odyssey.'"

"The moralities I have been desirous of inculcating in 'Atala' are easily discoverable, and as they are summed up in the Epilogue, I need not speak of them here. I will merely say a word or two concerning Chactas, the lover of Atala.

"He is a savage more than half civilized, since he knows not only the living, but also the dead languages of Europe. He can therefore express himself in a mixed style, suitable to the line upon which he stands, between society and nature. This circumstance has given me some advantages, by permitting Chactas to speak as a savage in the description of manners, and as a European in the dramatic portions of the narrative. Without that the work must have been abandoned. If I had always made use of the Indian style, 'Atala' would have been Hebrew for the reader.

"As to the missionary, he is a simple priest, who speaks without blushing of the Cross, of the blood of his Divine Master, of the corrupted flesh, etc.; in one word, he is really a priest. I am aware that it is difficult to depict such a character without awakening ideas of ridicule in the minds of certain readers. Where I do not draw a tear, I may raise a smile; that must depend upon individual sentiment."

"I must say a last word as to 'Atala.' The subject is not entirely of my invention. It is certain that there was a savage at the galleys and at the court of Louis XIV.; it is certain that a French missionary accomplished the facts I have related; it is certain that I saw savages in the American forests carrying away the bones of their forefathers, and a young mother exposing the body of her child upon the branches of a tree. Some other circumstances narrated are also veritable, but as they are not of general interest, it is needless for me to speak of them."

[From the Preface to "Alain" and "René" published in 1805.]

"I have been stopped in the corrections neither by the consideration of the cost of the book, nor by that of the length of the work. A few years have sufficed to make me acquainted with the weak or defective portions of that episode. Obedient upon this point to the critics, even so far as to reproach myself with an excess of docility, I have proved to those who attacked me that I never remain voluntarily in error, and that, at all times and upon all subjects, I am ready to give way to lights superior to my own. 'Atala' has been reprinted eleven times — five times separately and six times in the 'Genius of Christianity.' If those eleven editions were compared, scarcely two would be found to be altogether alike.

"The twelfth, which I now publish, has been revised with the greatest care. I have consulted the friends prompt to censure me; I have weighed each phrase, examined every word. The style, freed from certain epithets which embarrassed it, proceeds perhaps more naturally and with greater simplicity. I have introduced more order and logic into certain ideas, and I have effaced even the slightest inaccuracies of language. M. de la Harpe observed to me, on the subject of 'Atala,' 'If you will shut yourself up with me only for a few hours, that time will suffice for wiping out the spots that cause your critics to cry out so loudly.' I have passed four years in the revision of this episode; but it is now as I intend it to remain. It is at present the only 'Atala' I shall ever in future acknowledge."

"The new nature and the new manners I have described have also drawn upon me another ill-considered reproach. I have been taken for the inventor of certain extraordinary details, whereas I merely repeated circumstances well known to all travellers. Some notes added to the present edition of 'Atala' would easily have justified this assertion; but if I had introduced them at every point where each reader might have looked for them, they would soon have exceeded the length of the work itself. I therefore gave up the idea of annotations."

PROLOGUE

France formerly possessed in North America a vast empire, extending from Labrador to the Floridas, and from the shores of the Atlantic to the most distant lakes of Upper Canada.

Four great rivers, deriving their sources from the same mountains, divided these immense regions: the river St. Lawrence, which is lost to the east in the gulf of that name; the Western River, whose waters flow on to seas unknown; the river Bourbon, which runs from south to north into Hudson's Bay; and the Mississippi, whose waters fall from north to south into the Gulf of Mexico.

The last-named river, in its course of more than a thousand leagues, waters a delicious country, called by the inhabitants of the United States the New Eden, to which the French left the pretty appellation of Louisiana. A thousand other rivers, tributaries of the Mississippi—the Missouri, the Illinois, the Arkansas, the Wabache, the Tennessee—enrich it with their mud and fertilize it with their waters. When all these rivers have been swollen by the deluges of winter, uprooted trees, forming large portions of forests torn down by tempests, crowd about their sources. In a short time the mud cements the torn trees together, and they become enchained by creepers, which, taking root in every direction, bind and consolidate the débris. Carried away by the foaming waves, the rafts descend to the Mississippi, which, taking possession of them, hurries them down towards the Gulf of Mexico, throws them upon sandbanks, and so increases the number of its mouths. At intervals the swollen river raises its voice whilst passing over the resisting heaps, and spreads its overflowing waters around the colonnades of the forests, and the pyramids of the Indian tombs: and so the Mississippi is the Nile of these deserts. But grace is always united to splendor in the scenes of Nature: while the mid-stream bears away towards the sea the dead trunks of pine-trees and oaks, the lateral currents on either side convey along the shores floating islands of pistias and nenuphars, whose yellow roses stand out like little pavilions. Green serpents, blue herons, pink flamingoes, and baby crocodiles embark as passengers on these rafts of flowers; and the brilliant colony, unfolding to the wind its golden sails, glides along slumberingly till it arrives at some retired creek in the river.

The two shores of the Mississippi present the most extraordinary picture. On the western border vast savannahs spread away farther than the eye can reach, and their waves of verdure, as they recede, appear to rise gradually into the azure sky, where they fade away. In these limitless meadows herds of three or four thousand wild buffaloes wander at random. Sometimes, cleaving the waters as it swims, a bison, laden with years, comes to repose among the high grass on an island of the Mississippi, its forehead ornamented with two crescents, and its ancient and slimy beard giving it the appearance of a god of the river throwing an eye of satisfaction upon the grandeur of its waters, and the wild abundance of its shores.

"At intervals the swollen river raises its voice whilst passing over the resisting heaps,"

Such is the scene upon the western border; but it changes on the opposite side, which forms an admirable contrast with the other shore. Suspended along the course of the waters, grouped upon the rocks and upon the mountains, and dispersed in the valleys, trees of every form, of every color, and of every perfume, throng and grow together, stretching up into the air to heights that weary the eye to follow. Wild vines, bignonias, coloquintidas, intertwine each other at the feet of these trees, escalade their trunks, and creep along to the extremity of their branches, stretching from the maple to the tulip-tree, from the tulip-tree to the holly-hock, and thus forming thousands of grottoes, arches and porticoes. Often, in their wanderings from tree to tree, these creepers cross the arm of a river, over which they throw a bridge of flowers. Out of the midst of these masses, the magnolia, raising its motionless cone, surmounted by large white buds, commands all the forest, where it has no other rival than the palm-tree, which gently waves, close by, its fans of verdure.

A multitude of animals, placed in these retreats by the hand of the Creator, spread about life and enchantment. From the extremities of the avenues may be seen bears, intoxicated with the grape, staggering upon the branches of the elm-trees; cariboos bathe in the lake; black-squirrels play among the thick foliage; mocking-birds, and Virginian pigeons not bigger than sparrows, fly down upon the turf, reddened with strawberries; green parrots with yellow heads, purple woodpeckers, cardinals red as fire, clamber up to the very tops of the cypress-trees; humming-birds sparkle upon the jessamine of the Floridas; and bird-catching serpents hiss while suspended to the domes of the woods, where they swing about like the creepers themselves.

If all is silence and repose in the savannahs on the other side of the river, all here, on the contrary, is sound and motion; peckings against the trunks of the oaks, frictions of animals walking along as they nibble or crush between their teeth the stones of fruits, the roaring of the waves, plaintive cries, dull bellowings and mild cooings, fill these deserts with a tender yet wild harmony. But when a breeze happens to animate these solitudes, to swing these floating bodies, to confound these masses of white, blue, green, and pink, to mix all the colors and to combine all the murmurs, there issue such sounds from the depths of the forests, and such things pass before the eyes, that I should in vain endeavor to describe them to those who have never visited these primitive fields of Nature.

After the discovery of the Mississippi by Father Marquette and the unfortunate La Salle, the first Frenchmen who established themselves at Biloxi and at New Orleans entered into an alliance with the Natchez, an Indian nation whose power was redoubtable in those countries. Quarrels and jealousies subsequently ensanguined the land of hospitality. Amongst these savages there was an old man named Chactas,[1] who, on account of his age, wisdom and knowledge of the affairs of life, was the patriarch and the beloved of the deserts. Like many other men, he had acquired virtue by calamity. Not only were the forests of the New World filled with his misfortunes, but he bore the tale of his calamities even to the shores of France. Kept at the galleys at Marseilles by a cruel act of injustice, restored to liberty, and presented to Louis XIV., he had conversed with the great men of that age, and had been present at the fêtes of Versailles, at the tragedies of Racine, and at the funeral orations of Bossuet: in one word, the savage had contemplated society at the moment of its greatest splendor.

For several years Chactas, restored to the bosom of his country, had been in the enjoyment of repose. Nevertheless, Providence granted him even this favor dearly: the old man had become blind. A young girl used to accompany him on the hills of the Mississippi, just as Antigone formerly guided the steps of Odipus over

[1] The harmonious voice.

the Cithæron, or as Malvina conducted Ossian over the rocks of Morven.

In spite of the numerous acts of injustice to which Chactas had been subjected by the French, he was very partial to them. He ever remembered Fénélon, whose guest he had been, and desired an opportunity for rendering service to the fellow-countrymen of that virtuous man. A favorable occasion presented itself. In 1725 a Frenchman named René, driven thither by his passions and his misfortunes, arrived at Louisiana. He ascended the Mississippi as far as the territory of the Natchez, and asked to be accepted as a warrior of that nation. Chactas, having questioned him, and finding him not to be shaken in his resolution, adopted him as a son, and united him to an Indian girl called Céluta. Shortly after this marriage the savages prepared to go beaver-hunting.

On account of the respect with which the Indian tribes regarded the old man, Chactas, although blind, was appointed by the council of the wise men to command the expedition. Prayers and fasts commenced, the jugglers interpreted the dreams, the manitous were consulted, sacrifices of tobacco were offered up, fillets of elk-tongues were burnt, the assistants examining whether they sputtered in the flames, in order to ascertain the will of the genii; and at length they started, after having partaken of the sacred dog. René was of the party.

With the assistance of the counter-currents, the pirogues reascended the Mississippi, and reached the bed of the Ohio. One moonlight night, while all the Natchez were asleep at the bottom of their pirogues, and the Indian fleet, under a crowd of beast-skin sails, was flying before a mild breeze, René, who had remained alone with Chactas, asked him to tell the story of his adventures. The old man consented to satisfy his curiosity, and began in these words: —

"In these limitless meadows herds of three or four thousand wild buffaloes wander at random,"

CHACTAS' STORY

I.

THE HUNTERS.

The destiny which has brought us together, my dear son, is a singular one. I see in you the civilized man become savage: you see in me the wild man whom the Great Spirit (I know not from what motive) desired to civilize. Having each entered upon the career of life from opposite directions, you came to repose yourself at my place, and I have seated myself in yours; so that we must have acquired a totally different view of things. Which of the twain has gained or lost the more by this change of position? That is known to the genii, the least learned of whom possesses more wisdom than all mankind together.

"At the next flower-moon[2] there will be seven times ten snows, and three snows more, since my mother brought me into the world on the banks of the Mississippi. The Spaniards had recently established themselves in the Bay of Pensacola, but no European yet inhabited Louisiana. I had scarcely witnessed sev-

____

[2] The month of May.

enteen falls of the leaves when I marched with my father, the warrior Outalissi, against the Muscogulges, a powerful nation in the Floridas. We united our forces with those of the Spaniards, our allies, and the combat took place upon one of the branches of the Mobile. Areskoui[3] and the manitous were not favorable to us. Our enemies triumphed: my father lost his life; I was twice wounded whilst defending him. O why did I not then go down into the land of souls! I should have avoided the misfortunes which were awaiting me on earth. The Spirits ordained otherwise. I was dragged along by the defeated crowd to Saint Augustine.

"In that city, but then recently built by the Spaniards, I ran the risk of being carried away to the mines of Mexico, when an old Castilian, named Lopez, touched by my youth and simplicity, offered me an asylum, and presented me to his sister, with whom he was living spouseless.

"Both of them took to me in the tenderest manner. I was brought up with much care, and had all sorts of masters given to me. But after having passed thirty moons at Saint Augustine, I was afflicted with a disgust for the life of cities. I fell away visibly: sometimes I remained motionless for hours whilst contemplating the summits of distant forests; at other times I might be seen seated on the banks of a river, gazing sadly upon the flowing waters. I figured to myself the woods through which those waters had passed, and my soul was thus entirely given up to solitude.

"No longer able to resist the desire of returning to the desert, I one morning presented myself to Lopez dressed in my savage attire, holding in one hand my bow and arrows, and in the other my European costume, which I returned to my generous protector, at whose feet I fell, shedding a torrent of tears, giving myself odious names, and accusing myself of ingratitude. 'After all, O my father,' said I to him, 'you see it yourself; I must die if I do not resume the life of the Indian.'

"Lopez, struck with astonishment, endeavored to change my determination. He spoke of the dangers I was about to encounter, by exposing myself to the possibility of falling into the hands of the Muscogulges. But perceiving at last that I was resolved to risk everything, he melted into tears, and, pressing me in his arms with affection, 'Go,' said he, 'child of Nature; take back this independence of man, of which Lopez does not wish to deprive you. If I were myself younger, I would accompany you to the desert (where I also have sweet remembrances), and restore you to your mother's arms. When you shall be once again in your forests, think sometimes of the old Spaniard who gave you hospitality, and remember, in order that you may be disposed to love your fellow-creatures, that your first experience of the human heart was altogether in its favor.' Lopez finished by a prayer to the God of the Christians, whose religion I had refused to embrace, and we separated with much sadness.

"It was not long before I was punished for my ingratitude. My inexperience caused me to lose myself in the wood, and I was taken by a party of Muscogulges and Seminoles, as Lopez had predicted. My dress, and the feathers ornamenting my head, caused me to be recognized as a Natchez.

---

[3] The God of war.

"Trees of every form, of every color, and of every perfume,"

"All here, on the contrary, is sound and motion,"

I was enchained, but slightly, on account of my youth. Simaghan, the leader of the troop, desired to learn my name. I replied, 'I am called Chactas, son of Outalissi, son of Miscou, who have taken more than a hundred scalps from the heroes of the Muscogulges.' Simaghan then said, 'Chactas, son of Outalissi, son of Miscou, rejoice; thou shalt be burnt at the big village.' I answered, 'That is well,' and began to chaunt the song of death.

"Although a prisoner, I could not refrain, during the first few days, from admiring my enemies. The Muscogulge, and especially his ally, the Seminole, is full of gaiety, love and contentment. His walk is light, his mien calm and open. He speaks much, and with volubility. His language is harmonious and flowing. Even age does not deprive the sachems of this joyous simplicity: like the old birds of our forests, they mingle their ancient songs with the fresh notes of their young posterity.

"The women who accompanied the troop displayed for my youth a tender pity and an amiable curiosity. They questioned me about my mother, concerning the earliest days of my life; and they wanted to know whether my cradle of moss had been hung upon the flowering branches of the maple-trees, and whether the breezes had rocked me near the nests of the little birds. Then came a thousand other questions as to the state of my heart. They asked me if I had seen a white fawn in my dreams, and whether the trees of the secret valley had advised me to love. I replied with simplicity to the mothers, to the daughters, and to the spouses of the men, saying, 'You are the graces of the day, and the night loves you like dew. Man issues from your loins to hang upon your breast and upon your lips: you know the magic words that lull every pain. So was I told by her who brought me into the world, and who will never see me again! She told me also that maidens are mysterious flowers met with in solitary places.'

"These praises gave much pleasure to the women, who overwhelmed me with all sorts of presents, and brought me cocoa-nut cream, maple-tree sugar, sagan-rite,[4] bear-hams, beaver-skins, shells with which to ornament myself, and moss for my couch. They sang and laughed with me, and then took to shedding tears at the thought that I was to be burnt.

"One night, when the Muscogulges had pitched their camp on the outskirt of a forest, I was seated near the war-fire with the guard who had charge of me. All of a sudden, I heard the sound of a dress upon the grass, and a female, half-veiled, came and sat down by my side. Tears were rolling from beneath her eyelids, and I saw by the light of the fire that a small golden crucifix shone upon her bosom. She was altogether beautiful, and I remarked upon her countenance an expression of virtue and passion of irresistible attraction. To that she added the most tender graces: an extreme sensitiveness, united to a profound melancholy, breathed in her looks, and her smile was heavenly.

"I took her to be the Virgin of the last Loves, the virgin sent to the prisoner of war to enchant his tomb. Under this impression, I said to her stammeringly, and with an emotion that did not, however, proceed from any feeling of fear of the funeral pile, 'O virgin, you are worthy of a first love, and you are not made for the last. The palpitations of a heart that will soon cease to beat would ill respond to the movements of your own. How can death and life lie mingled together? You would cause me to regret too much the approach of day. Let another be happier than myself, and may long embraces unite the tender plant to the oak!'

"The youthful maiden then said to me, 'I am not the Virgin of the last Loves. Are you a Christian?' I replied that I had not betrayed the genii of my cottage. At these words the Indian made an involuntary movement, and said, 'I pity you for being merely a wicked idolator. My mother made me a Christian; my name is Atala, and I am the daughter of Simaghan of the Golden Bracelets, the chief of the warriors of this troop. We are going to Apalachucla, where you will be burnt.' Having uttered these words, Atala rose and took her departure."

---

[4] A description of cake made with Indian corn.

Here. Chactas was compelled to interrupt his story. A crowd of souvenirs rushed into his soul; his closed eyes inundated his furrowed cheeks with tears, just as two springs, hidden in the profound depths of the earth, reveal themselves by the waters they send filtering between the rocks.

"Oh, my son," said he, after a long pause, "you perceive that Chactas is not very wise, notwithstanding his reputation for wisdom. Alas! my dear child, although men can no longer see, they can still weep! Several days passed. Every evening the old man's daughter came to converse with me. Sleep had fled from my eyes, and Atala was in my heart like the remembrance of the resting-place of my fathers.

"On the seventeenth day of our march, about the time when the ephemeran rises from the waters, we entered upon the grand savannah of Alachua. The plain is surrounded with hills, which, receding behind one another, are covered, as they appear to touch the clouds, with ranges of forests of palm-trees, citron-trees, magnolias and oaks. The chief uttered the cry of arrival, and the troop encamped at the foot of a hill-side. I was left at some distance, on the border of one of those natural wells so famous in the Floridas, attached to the trunk of a tree, and guarded by a warrior who watched me with impatience. I had passed but some moments in this place when Atala appeared beneath the liquid ambers of the fountain. 'Hunter,' said she to the Muscogulgan hero, 'if you would like to chase the stag, I will guard the prisoner.' The warrior jumped for joy at this offer of the chiefs daughter, and at once hurried from the top of the hill, and directed his steps towards the plain.

"What a strange contradiction is the heart of man! I, who had so much desired to speak of things mysterious to her whom I already loved like the sun, suddenly became troubled and confused, and felt as though I should have preferred to be thrown amongst the crocodiles in the fountain to finding myself alone with Atala. The daughter of the desert was as much affected as her prisoner. We observed a profound silence; for the genii of love had deprived us of speech. After an interval, Atala, making an effort, spoke thus: 'Warrior, you are held but slightly: you can easily escape.' At these words courage returned to my tongue, and I replied, 'But slightly held, O woman!' — — I could not complete my phrase. Atala hesitated some moments, and then said, 'Fly!' at the same time liberating me from the trunk of the tree. I seized the cord, and returned it to the hand of the foreign maiden, forcing her beautiful fingers to close themselves upon my chain. 'Take it back! Take it back!' I cried. 'You are mad!' said Atala, in a voice full of emotion. 'Wretched man, do you not know that you will be burnt? What do you mean? Do you reflect that I am the daughter of a redoubtable sachem?' 'There was a time,' I replied, with tears, 'when I also was carried about in a beaver-skin on the shoulders of a mother: my father also had a fine cottage, and his fawns drank of the waters of a thousand torrents; but I now wander without a country. When I shall have ceased to exist, no friend will place a little grass over my body, to keep the insects away from it. The corpse of an unhappy stranger interests no one.'

"These words touched Atala. Her tears fell into the fountain. 'Ah,' I continued with vivacity, 'if your heart spoke like mine! Is not the desert free? Do not the forests contain folds in which we could conceal ourselves? And, in order to be happy, are there so many things necessary for the children of the huts? O maiden, more beautiful than the first dream of a spouse! O my well-beloved, dare to follow me!' Such was my language. Atala replied to me in a tender tone of voice, 'My young friend, you have learnt the expressions of the white men; it is easy to deceive an Indian girl!' 'What!' I exclaimed, 'you call me your young friend. Ah, if a poor slave' — — 'Well,' said she, leaning upon me, 'a poor slave' — —

I continued with ardor, 'Let a kiss assure him of your faith!' Atala listened to my prayers. As a fawn appears to cling to the flowers of the rosy creepers which it seizes with its delicate tongue on the mountain-steeps, so I remained attached to the lips of my well-beloved.

"The combat took place upon one of the branches of the mobile,"

"Alas, my dear son, pain is in close attendance upon pleasure. Who could have thought that the moment in which Atala gave me the first token of her love should be precisely that in which she would destroy all my hopes? White hairs of old Chactas, what was your astonishment when the daughter of the sachem pronounced these words: 'Beautiful prisoner, I have foolishly given way to your desire; but whither will this passion lead us? My religion separates me from you for ever— —. Oh, my mother, what hast thou done?'— — Atala became suddenly silent, and kept back I know not what fatal secret about to escape from her lips. Her words plunged me into despair. 'Well, then,' I exclaimed, 'I will be as cruel as you; I will not escape. You shall see me in the flame of fire; you shall hear the groans of my flesh, and you will be full of joy.' Atala took my hands between both of hers. 'Poor young idolator,' she cried, 'I really grieve for you! You wish me, then, to weep my whole heart out? What a pity I cannot fly with you! Unhappy was the bosom of thy mother, O Atala! Why dost thou not throw thyself to the crocodiles in the fountain?'

"That very moment the crocodiles, at the approach of the setting of the sun, began to make their cries heard. Atala said to me, 'Let us leave this place.' I led away the daughter of Simaghan to the foot of the hills, which form gulfs of verdure by advancing their promontories into the savannahs. Everything in the desert was splendidly imposing. The stork was screaming upon its nest; the woods resounded with the monotonous song of the quails, the whistling of the paraquets, the lowing of the bisons and the neighing of the Siminolian cavalry.

"Our promenade was almost a dumb one. I walked by the side of Atala, who was holding the end of the cord which I had forced her to take back again. Sometimes we shed tears, and sometimes we endeavored to smile. A look, now directed towards the sky and then towards the earth; an ear listening to the song of the birds; a gesture towards the setting sun; a hand tenderly pressed; a bosom by turns palpitating and tranquil: the names of Chactas and Atala softly repeated at intervals! Oh, first promenade of love, thy souvenir must be extremely powerful, since after so many years of misfortune it can still stir the heart of old Chactas!

"How incomprehensible are mortals when agitated by the passions! I had just abandoned the generous-hearted Lopez; I had just exposed myself to every danger for the sake of liberty, and in one instant the look of a woman had changed my tastes, my resolutions, my thoughts! Forgetful of my country, my mother, my cabin, and the frightful death awaiting me, I had become indifferent to everything that was not Atala. Lacking strength to raise myself to the reason of a man, I had suddenly fallen into a sort of childishness, and, far from being able to do anything to extricate myself from threatening misfortunes, I almost required some one to provide me with the means of sleep and nourishment.

"It was therefore in vain that Atala, after our ramble in the savannah, threw herself at my knees and again begged me to leave her. I declared that I would return alone to the camp, if she refused to re-attach me to the trunk of my tree. She was compelled to comply with my request, hoping to convince me another time.

"The next day, which decided the fate of my life, we halted in a valley not far from Cuscowilla, the capital of the Seminoles. These Indians, together with the

Muscogulges, form the confederation of the Creeks. The daughter of the land of palm-trees came to find me in the middle of the night. She conducted me to a great pine-forest, and renewed her entreaties to induce me to escape. Without replying to her, I took her hand in mine, and forced the thirsting fawn to wander with me into the forest. The night was delicious. The genius of the air appeared to be shaking the blue canopy, embalmed with the odor of the pines; and we breathed a slight perfume of amber emitted by the crocodiles asleep beneath the tamarind-trees by the river-side. The moon was shining in the midst of a spotless azure, and the pearl-grey light fell upon the undefined summit of the forests. Not a sound was to be heard, except I know not what distant harmony that reigned in the depth of the woods. It seemed as though the soul of solitude was sighing throughout the entire extent of the desert.

"Through the trees we perceived a young man, who, holding a torch in his hand, looked like the genius of spring visiting the forests to reanimate Nature. He was a lover on his way to learn his fate at the cabin of his mistress.

"Should the maiden blow out the torch, she accepts the offered vows; but if she veil herself without extinguishing it, she refuses the spouse.

"The warrior, gliding through the shades, chanted these words in a low tone of voice:

"'I will outrun the steps of the daylight upon the mountain-tops to seek my lonely dove in the midst of the oaks of the forest.

"'I have fastened around her throat a necklace of porcelain,[5] with three red beads for my love, three violet ones for my fears, three blue ones for my hopes.

"'Mila has the eyes of an ermine, and hair as light as a field of rice; her mouth is a pink shell lined with pearls; her two breasts are like two little spotless kids, born the same day of one mother.

---

[5] A necklace of shells.

"All of a sudden, I heard the sound of a dress upon the grass,"

"'May Mila extinguish this torch! May her mouth cast a voluptuous shade over it! I will fertilize her bosom! The hope of the country shall hang from her fruitful breast, and I will smoke my calumet of peace by the cradle of my son.

"'Ah! let me outrun the steps of the daylight upon the mountain-tops to seek my lonely dove amidst the oaks of the forest!'

"Thus sang this young man, whose accents agitated me to the bottom of my soul, and caused Atala to chance countenance. Our united hands trembled in each other. But we were diverted from this scene by another scene not less dangerous for us.

"We passed near a child's tomb, which served as a boundary between two nations. It had been placed on the border of the road, according to custom, in order that the young wives, when going to the fountain, might draw into their bosom the soul of the innocent creature, and restore it to the country. At this moment several newly-married spouses were there, and, desirous of the sweets of maternity, were endeavoring, by opening their lips, to receive the soul of the little child, which they fancied they saw wandering amongst the flowers. The veritable mother came afterwards, and deposited a bunch of corn and white lilies upon the tomb; she sprinkled the earth with her milk, sat down upon the damp turf, and spoke thus to her child in an impassioned voice:

"'Why do I weep for thee in thy earthly cradle, O my new-born? When the little bird has grown, it must seek its own nutriment, and finds many bitter seeds in the desert. At least thou hast been unconscious of tears; at least thy heart has not been exposed to the devouring breath of men. The bud that dries up in its envelope passes away with all its perfumes, like thou, O my son, with all thine innocence. Happy are those who die in the cradle! they have only known the kisses and smiles of a mother!'

"Already subdued by our own hearts, we were overwhelmed by the images of love and maternity which seemed to pursue us in these enchanted solitudes. I carried Atala away in my arms to the extremity of the forest, where I told her things that I should in vain endeavor to repeat to-day with my lips. The southern wind, my dear son, loses its heat on passing over mountains of ice. The souvenirs of love in the heart of an old man are like the fires of day reflected by the peaceful orb of the moon when the sun has set, and silence spreads itself over the huts of the savages.

"What could save Atala? what could prevent her from succumbing to Nature? Nothing, doubtless, but a miracle; and that miracle was accomplished. The daughter of Simaghan had recourse to the God of the Christians; she threw herself upon the ground, and uttered a fervent prayer, addressed to her mother and to the Queen of Virgins. It was from this moment, O René, that I entertained a wonderful idea of that religion which, in the forests, in the midst of all the privations of life, imparts a thousand boons to the unfortunate; of that religion which, opposing its power to the torrent of the passions, suffices alone to conquer them, when everything else is in their favor—the secrecy of the woods, the absence of men, and the fidelity of the shades. Ah, how divine to me appeared that simple savage, the ignorant Atala, who, on her knees before an old fallen pine-tree, as at the foot of an altar, was offering up a prayer to her God in favor of an idolatrous lover! Her eyes raised towards the star of the night, her cheeks, brilliant with tears of religion and of love, were of immortal beauty. Several times it appeared to me as though she were about to take her flight to heaven; several times I fancied I saw come down upon the rays of the moon, and heard amidst the trees, those genii whom the God of the Christians sends to the hermits of the rocks when He is about to call them back to Himself. I was afflicted by all this, for I feared that Atala had but little time to remain on earth.

"Nevertheless, she shed such abundant tears, she appeared so unhappy, that

I was perhaps upon the point of consenting to take my departure, when the cry of death resounded through the forest. Four armed men rushed upon me. We had been discovered; the war-chief had given orders for our pursuit.

"Atala, who resembled a queen in the pride of her demeanor, disdained to speak to these warriors. She glanced nobly at them, and went forthwith to Simaghan.

"She could obtain no concession. My guards were doubled, my chains increased, and my lover was kept away from me. Five nights passed, and then we perceived Apalachucla, situated on the banks of the river Chata-Uche. I was immediately crowned with flowers; my face was painted blue and red; beads were fastened to my nose and to my ears, and a chichikoué[6] was placed in my hand.

"Thus prepared for the sacrifice, I entered Apalachucla amidst the reiterated shouts of the crowd. My fate was sealed; when all of a sudden the sound of a conch was heard, and the mico, or chief of the nation, ordered an assembly.

"You know, my son, the torments to which savages subject their prisoners of war. Christian missionaries, at the risk of their lives, and with an indefatigable charity, had succeeded in inducing several nations to substitute a comparatively mild slavery to the horrors of the funeral pile. The Muscogulges had not yet adopted this custom, but a numerous party amongst them had declared themselves in favor of it. It was to decide upon this important matter that the mico had convoked the sachems, or wise men. I was conducted to the place of deliberation.

"The pavilion of the council was situated upon an isolated mound not far from Apalachucla. Three circles of columns constituted the elegant architecture of this rotunda. The columns were of polished and carved cypress-wood, increasing in height and in thickness, and diminishing in number as they approached the centre, which was indicated by a single pillar. From the summit of this pillar depended strips of bark, which, passing over the tops of the other columns, covered the pavilion in the guise of an open fan.

"The council assembled. Fifty old men, in beaver cloaks, were ranged upon the steps facing the door of the pavilion. The grand chief was seated in their midst, holding in his hand the calumet of peace, half-colored for war. On the right of the old men were placed fifty women, dressed in robes of swan-feathers. The war-chiefs, with a tomahawk in the hand, a bunch of feathers on the head, and their arms and chests dyed with blood, occupied the left.

"At the foot of the central column the fire of the council was burning. The first jungler, surrounded by eight guardians of the temple, dressed in long vestments, and wearing a stuffed owl upon their heads, poured some balm of copal upon the flames, and offered a sacrifice to the sun. The triple row of old men, matrons, and warriors—the priests, the clouds of incense, and the sacrifice—imparted to this council an aspect altogether imposing.

---

[6] A musical instrument played by the savages.

"Several times it appeared to me as though she were about to take her flight to heaven,"

"I was standing chained in the midst of the assembly. When the sacrifice was finished, the mico spoke, and explained with simplicity the affair that had brought the council together. He threw a blue necklace upon the ground, as evidence of what he had just said.

"Then a sachem of the tribe of the Eagle rose, and spoke thus:

"'My father the mico, sachems, matrons, warriors of the four tribes of the Eagle, the Beaver, the Serpent, and the Tortoise, let us change nothing in the manners of our forefathers: let us burn the prisoner, and let us not allow our courage to be weakened. It is a custom of the white men that is now proposed to you; it cannot be other than pernicious. Give a red collar which contains my words. I have spoken.'

"And he threw a red collar into the midst of the assembly.

"A matron then rose, and said:

"'My father Eagle, you have the cleverness of a fox and the prudent slowness of a tortoise. I will polish the chain of friendship with you, and we will plant together the tree of peace. But let us change the customs of our forefathers when they are of a terrible character. Let us have slaves to cultivate our fields, and let us no longer hear the cries of the prisoners, which trouble the bosoms of the mothers. I have spoken.'

"As the waves of the ocean are broken up by a storm; as in autumn the dried leaves are carried away in a whirlwind; as the reeds of the Mississippi bend and rise again during a sudden inundation; as a great herd of deer bellow in the depths of a forest, so was the council agitated and murmuring. Sachems, warriors, and matrons spoke by turns, or all together. Interests clashed, opinions were divided, and the council was about to be dissolved; but at length the ancient custom prevailed, and I was condemned to the pile.

"A circumstance caused my punishment to be delayed: the Feast of the Dead, or the Festival of Souls, was approaching, and it is the custom not to put any captive to death during the days consecrated to that ceremony. I was handed over to a strict guard, and doubtless the sachems had sent away the daughter of Simaghan, as I saw her no longer.

"Meanwhile, the tribes for more than three hundred leagues around came in crowds to celebrate the Festival of Souls. A long hut had been constructed upon an isolated situation. On the day indicated, each cabin exhumed the remains of its fathers from their private tombs, and the skeletons were hung upon the walls of the Common-room of the Ancestors in order and by families. The winds (a tempest had burst forth), the forests, and the cataracts roared from without, while the old men of the different nations were engaged in concluding treaties of peace between the tribes over the bones of their fathers.

"Funeral amusements were indulged in, running, ball, and a game with small bones. Two maidens tried to snatch from each other a willow-twig. Their hands fluttered about the twig, which each in her turn held above her head. Their beautiful naked feet intertwined, their mouths met, their sweet breaths became confounded; they stooped, and their hairs were mixed together; then they looked at their mothers, and blushed in the midst of applause.[7] The jungler invoked Michabou, the genius of the waters, and related the wars of the great Hare against Machimanitou, the god of evil. He spoke of the first man, and of Athaënsic, the first woman, being hurled from heaven for having lost their innocence; of the earth having been reddened with a brother's blood; of the immolation of Tahouistsarou by the impious Jouskeka; of the deluge commanded by the voice of the Great Spirit; of Massou, the only one saved in his bark vessel; and of the crow sent out to discover the land. He spoke, moreover, of the beautiful Endaë, recalled from the land of souls by the sweet songs of her spouse.

[7] Blushing is a marked characteristic with young savages.

"After these games and hymns, preparations were made for giving the ancestors an eternal sepulture.

"Upon the borders of the river Chata-Uche there was a wild fig-tree, which the worship of the people had consecrated. The Indian maidens were in the habit of washing their bark-dresses at this place, and exposing them to the breath of the desert upon the branches of the ancient tree. It was there that an immense tomb had been dug.

"While leaving the funeral chamber, the hymn of death was sung. Each family carried some sacred remains. On arriving at the tomb, the relics were lowered down into it, and spread out in layers, separated by the skins of bears and beavers; the mound of the tomb was then raised, and the tree of tears and of sleep planted upon it.

"Let us pity men, my dear son! Those very Indians whose customs are so touching, those very women who had displayed such a tender interest in my behalf, now called out loudly for my execution; and entire tribes delayed their departure, in order to have the pleasure of seeing a young man undergo the most horrible sufferings.

"In a valley to the north, at some distance from the grand village, was a wood of cypresses and deals, called the Wood of Blood. It was reached by the ruins of one of those monuments of which the origin is ignored, and which were the work of a people now unknown. I was led thither in triumph. Preparations were being made for my death. The pole of Areskoui was planted; pine, elm, and cypress-trees fell beneath the axe; the funeral pile was rising, and spectators were constructing amphitheatres with the branches and trunks of trees. Each one was occupied in inventing a torture. Some proposed to tear the skin off my head, others to burn my eyes out with red-hot axes. I began to sing the song of death:

"'I do not fear torture: I am brave, O Muscognlges! I defy you; I despise you more than women. My father, Outalissi, son of Miscou, drank out of the skulls of your most famous warriors; you will not draw a sigh from my breast.'

"Provoked by my song, a warrior pierced my arm with an arrow. I merely said, 'Brother, I thank thee.'

"In spite of the activity of the executioners, the preparations for my execution could not be completed before the setting of the sun. A jungler was consulted, and he forbade the genii of the shades to be troubled, so that my death was postponed till the following day. But, in their impatience to enjoy the spectacle, and in order to be ready sooner on the break of day, the Indians did not quit the Wood of Blood. They lighted large fires, and began a series of festivities and dances.

"It was reached by the ruins of one of those monuments of which the origin is ignored,"

"Meanwhile, I had been laid down upon my back. Cords from my neck, from my feet, and from my arms, were attached to stakes fixed in the ground. Warriors were seated upon these cords, and I could not make the slightest movement without their knowledge. The night advanced; the songs and dances gradually ceased; the fires emitted but a ruddy light, in front of which I could see the shadows of some of the savages pass. At last they all fell asleep; but as the noise of men became pacified, that of the desert seemed to increase, and to the tumult of voices succeeded the howlings of the winds in the forest.

"It was the hour when a young Indian recently become a mother awakes with a start in the middle of the night, fancying she has heard the cry of her first-born babe desirous of her sweet nutriment. With my eyes gazing up to heaven, where the crescent moon was wandering in the clouds, I was reflecting upon my destiny. Atala appeared to me to be a monster of ingratitude thus to abandon me at the moment of punishment—I, who had given myself up to the flames rather than leave her! And yet I felt that I still loved her, and that I should die with joy for Atala.

"In extreme pleasures there is a sting that excites one as though to counsel us to profit by the rapidly passing moment: in great grief, on the contrary, there is something heavy that induces drowsiness; the eyes fatigued with tears naturally seek to close, and the goodness of Providence may be thus remarked even in our misfortunes. I gave way, in spite of myself, to that heavy sleep which sometimes overcomes the wretched. I dreamt that my chains were being taken off; I thought I felt the satisfaction experienced when, after having been tightly pressed, a helping hand relieves us of our irons.

"This sensation was so vivid that it caused me to raise my eyelids. By the light of the moon, a ray of which was escaping between two clouds, I saw a tall white figure leaning over me, and silently occupied in loosening my bonds. I was about to utter a cry, when a hand, which I instantly recognized, closed my mouth. A single cord remained, but it appeared impossible to cut it without touching a warrior who covered it entirely with his body. Atala placed her hand upon it. The warrior, half-awakened, bestirred himself, and sat up. Atala remained motionless, and looked at him. The Indian thought he was looking at the Spirit of the ruins; and he lay down again, closing his eyes and invoking his manitou. The bond was broken. I arose and followed my deliverer, who tendered to me the end of a bow of which she held the other extremity. But with what dangers were we surrounded! At times we were on the point of stumbling over the sleeping savages; then a guard questioned us, and Atala replied in an assumed voice. Children were crying, and dogs barking. Scarcely had we got clear of the fatal enclosure, when terrible howlings resounded through the forest. The camp was aroused. A thousand fires were lighted, and savages were running about in all directions with torches. We hurried away with precipitation.

"When day broke upon the Apalaches, we were already far away. Great was my felicity on finding myself again in solitude with Atala—with Atala my deliverer, with Atala who was giving herself to me for ever! Words failed my tongue. I fell on my knees, and said to the daughter of Simaghan: 'Men are but little; but when the genii visit them, they are nothing at all. You are a genius; you have visited me, and I cannot speak before you.' Atala offered me her hand with a smile: 'I am obliged to follow you,' she said, 'since you will not fly without me. During the night I seduced the jungler with presents, I intoxicated your executioners with essence of fire,[8] and I risked my life for you, because you had given yours for me. Yes, young idolator!' she added, with an accent that alarmed me, 'the sacrifice will be reciprocal.'

[8] Brandy.

"Atala gave me the weapons she had had the precaution to bring, and then she dressed my wound. Whilst wiping it with a papaya-leaf, she wetted it with her tears. 'It is a balm,' I said to her, 'that you are dropping on my arm.' 'I am rather afraid that it may be a poison,' she replied. She tore one of the coverings from her bosom, with which she made a first bandage that she fastened with a tress of lier hair.

"Intoxication, which lasts a long time upon savages, and is for them a species of malady, prevented them from pursuing us during the first few days. If they sought for us afterwards, it was probably in a westerly direction, as they must have thought we should make for the Mississippi; but we had taken our flight towards the fixed star,[9] guiding ourselves by the moss on the trunks of the trees.

"We were not long in perceiving that we had gained but little by my deliverance. The desert now unrolled before us its immeasurable solitudes. Without experience in forest life, having lost our way, and walking on at hazard, what was to become of us? Often, while gazing upon Atala, I remembered the ancient story of Agar, that Lopez had given me to read, and which happened in the desert of Beersheba a long time ago, when men lived to three times the age of the oak.

"Atala made me a cloak out of some ash-bark, and she also embroidered me a pair of musk rat skin moccasins with porcupine's hair. In my turn, I did all in my power to ornament her attire. First of all, I placed upon her head a crown of those blue mallows that crowded beneath our feet in the abandoned Indian cemeteries; then I made her necklaces of red azalea-berries; and after all I smiled in the contemplation of her wonderful beauty.

"When we encountered a river, we crossed it either on a raft or by swimming. Atala placed one of her hands upon my shoulder, and thus, like a pair of migratory swans, we traversed the solitary waves.

"During the great heat of the day we often sought shelter beneath the moss of the cedars. Nearly all the Floridan trees, especially the cedar and the oak, are covered with a white moss, which descends from their branches down to the very ground. At night-time, by moonlight, should you happen to see, in the open savannah, an isolated holm dressed in such drapery, you would imagine it to be a phantom dragging after it a number of long veils. The scene is not less picturesque by day, when a crowd of butterflies, brilliant insects, colibris, green paroquets, and blue jackdaws entangle themselves amongst the moss, and thus produce the effect of a piece of white woollen tapestry embroidered by some clever European workman with beautiful birds and sparkling insects.

---

[9] The north.

"At last they all fell asleep; but as the noise of men became pacified, that of the desert seemed to increase, and to the tumult of voices succeeded the howlings of the winds in the forest,"

"Great was my felicity on finding myself again in solitude with Atala,"

"It was in the shade of such smiling quarters, prepared by the Great Spirit, that we stopped to repose ourselves. When the winds come down from heaven to rock the great cedar, when the aerial castles built upon its brandies undulate with the birds and the travellers sleeping beneath its shelter, when thousands of sighs pass through the corridors of the waving edifice, there is nothing amongst the wonders of the ancient world to be compared with this monument of the desert.

"Every evening we lighted a large fire and built a travelling hut of bark raised upon four stakes. When I had killed a wild turkey, a pigeon, or a wood-pheasant, we attached it to the end of a pole before a pile of burning oak, and left the care of turning the hunter's prey to the caprices of the wind. We used to eat a kind of moss called rock-tripe, sweetened bark, and May-apples, that tasted of the peach and the raspberry. The black-walnut-tree, the maple-tree, and the sumach furnished our table with wine. Sometimes I went and fetched from amongst the reeds a plant whose flower, in the form of an elongated cup, contained a glass of the purest dew. We blessed Heaven for having placed this limpid spring upon the stalk of a flower, in the midst of the corrupted marshes, just as it has placed hope at the bottom of hearts ulcerated by grief; just also as it has caused virtue to well up from the bosom of the miseries of life!

"I soon discovered, alas! that I had deceived myself as to the apparent calm of my beloved Atala. The farther we advanced the sadder she became. She frequently shuddered without a cause, and turned her head aside hurriedly. I sometimes caught her regarding me with a passionate look, which she at once cast towards the sky with a profound melancholy. What alarmed me above all was a secret thought concealed in the bottom of her soul, but which I read in her eyes. Constantly drawing me towards her and then pushing me away, re-animating my hopes, and then destroying them when I thought I had made some progress in her heart, I found myself still at the same point. How many times she said to me, 'O my young sweetheart! I love you like the shade of the woods at mid-day!' You are as beautiful as the desert with all its flowers and all its breezes. If I incline towards you, I tremble: when my hand falls upon yours, it seems to me as though I were about to die. The other day the wind blew your hair upon my face as you were reposing yourself upon my bosom, and I fancied I felt the light touch of the invisible spirits. Yes, I have seen the young kids of the mountain of Occona; I have listened to the language of men ripe with years; but the mildness of goats and the wisdom of old men are less agreeable and less powerful than your words. Ah, my poor Chactas! I shall never be your spouse!'

"The constant struggle between Atala's love and religion, her tender freedom and the chastity of her conduct, the pride of her character and her profound sensitiveness, the elevation of her soul in great things, her susceptibility about trifles, rendered her, in my opinion, an incomprehensible being. Atala could not hold a weak empire over a man. Full of passion, she was full of power. She must either be adored or hated.

"After fifteen nights of hurried march, we entered upon the chain of the Alleghany mountains, and reached one of the branches of the Tennessee, a river that falls into the Ohio. Aided by the advice of Atala, I built a boat, which I coated with plum-tree gum, after having re-sewn the bark with roots of the fir. I subsequently embarked therein with Atala, and we abandoned ourselves to the current of the river.

"The Indian village of Sticoë, with its pyramidal tombs and ruined huts, appeared on our left at the turn of a promontory; on the right we left the valley of Keow, terminated by the perspective of the cabins of Jore, which seemed to be suspended from the forehead of the mountain of the same name. The river which carried us along flowed between high cliffs, at the extremity of which we perceived the setting sun. The profound solitudes were not disturbed by the presence of men. We only saw one Indian hunter, who, leaning motionless upon his bow, on the peak of a rock, looked like a statue raised upon the mountain to the genius of those deserts.

"Atala and myself added our silence to the silence of this scene. All of a sudden, the daughter of exile filled the air by thus singing, in a voice replete with melancholy emotion, of her absent country:

"'Happy are they who have not seen the smoke of foreign festivals, and who have never been seated elsewhere than at the rejoicings of their fathers!

"'If the blue jackdaw of the Mississippi were to say to the nonpareil of the Floridas, "Why dost thou complain so sadly? Hast thou not here beautiful waters and lovely shades, and all sorts of pastures, as in thine own forests?"

"Yes," would reply the fugitive nonpareil; "but my nest is in the jessamine; who will bring it to me? And the sun of my savannah, where is it?"

"'Happy are they who have not seen the smoke of foreign festivals, and who have never been seated elsewhere than at the rejoicings of their fathers!

"'After hours of painful wayfare, the traveller sits down in sadness. He sees around him the roofs of men's habitations, but has no place wherein to repose his head. The traveller knocks at a cabin, places his bow behind the door, and asks for hospitality. The master makes a gesture of the hand; the traveller takes back his bow, and returns to the desert.

"'Happy are they who have not seen the smoke of foreign festivals, and who have never been seated elsewhere than at the rejoicings of their fathers!

"'Wondrous stories told around the hearth, tender effusions of the heart, long habits of loving so necessary to life, you have filled the days of those who have not quitted their natal place! Their tombs are in the land of their birth, with the setting sun, the tears of their friends and the charms of religion.

"'Happy are they who have not seen the smoke of foreign festivals, and who have never been seated elsewhere than at the rejoicings of their fathers!'

"Thus sang Atala. Nothing interrupted the course of her lamentations, except the almost imperceptible sound of our boat upon the waves. In two or three places only were they taken up by a weak echo, which repeated them to a second, and the second to a third, faintly and more faintly still. It seemed as though the souls of two lovers, formerly unfortunate like ourselves, and attracted by the touching melody, were enjoying the pleasure of sighing forth the dying sounds of its music in the mountain.

"Nevertheless, the solitude, the constant presence of the beloved object, even our misfortunes, increased our affection from one instant to another. Atala prayed continuously to her mother, whose irritated shade she seemed as though wishing to appease. She sometimes asked me if I did not hear a plaintive voice, and see flames issuing out of the earth. As for myself, exhausted with fatigue, but still burning with desire, and thinking that I was perhaps irretrievably lost in the midst of those forests, I was a hundred times upon the point of drawing my spouse to my arms, and a hundred times did I urge Atala to allow me to build a hut upon the river side, so that we might bury ourselves therein together. But she always resisted my propositions. 'Remember, my young friend,' she would say, 'that a warrior owes himself to his country. What is a woman compared to the duties you have to fulfil? Take courage, son of Outalissi; do not murmur against your destiny. The heart of man is like a river-sponge, that imbibes pure water during calm weather, and is swollen with muddy liquid when the sky has troubled the waves. Has the sponge the right to say, "I thought there would never be any storms, and that the sun would never be scorching?"'

"O René, if you fear the trials of the heart, be upon your guard against solitude. The great passions are solitary, and to transport them to the desert is to restore them to their triumph. Overcome with cares and fears; exposed to the danger of falling into the hands of Indian enemies, to be swallowed up by the waters, stung by serpents, devoured by beasts; finding the poorest nourishment with difficulty, and not knowing whither to direct our steps, it seemed impossible for our misfortunes to be greater, when an accident brought them to a climax.

"It was the twenty-seventh sun since our departure from the cabins. The moon of fire[10] had commenced her course, and everything announced a storm. Towards the hour when the Indian matrons hang up the plough-handle to the branches of the sabin-tree, and when the paroquets retire into the hollows of the cypress, the sky began to be overcast. The voices of the solitude died away, the desert became silent, and the forests were reposing in the midst of a universal calm. Shortly after, the rollings of a distant thunder, prolonged through the woods as old as the world, re-issued from them with sublime sounds. Fearful of being submerged, we hastened to reach the bank of the river, and withdrew into a forest.

"The ground in this place was marshy. We advanced with difficulty under a vault of smilax, amidst vines, indigo-plants, bean-trees, and creeping ivy that entangled our feet like nets. The spongy soil trembled around us, and at each instant we were on the point of sinking into the quagmires. Insects without number, and enormous bats, blinded us; bell-serpents were hissing in every direction, and wolves, bears, carcajous, and young tigers, come to hide themselves in these retreats, made them resound with their roarings.

"Meanwhile, the darkness increased. The lowering clouds were entering beneath the leafy covering of the woods. Suddenly the sky was rent, and the lightning traced a rapid zig-zag of fire. A violent wind from the west rolled clouds upon clouds; the forests bent; the sky opened time after time, and from between the interstices other skies and ardent scenes might be perceived. What a frightful, what a magnificent spectacle! The lightning set fire to the forest; the conflagration extended like a head-dress of flame; columns of sparks and of smoke besieged the clouds, which were vomiting their flashes into the vast burning mass. Then the Great Spirit covered the mountain with heavy darkness; and from the midst of this chaos there arose a confused moaning, formed by the rushing of the winds, the cracking of trees, the howling of wild beasts, the buzzing of the inflamed vege-

[10] The month of July.

ATALA

tation, and the repeated fall of thunderbolts hissing as they died out in the waters.

"The Great Spirit knows that at this moment I saw and thought of nothing but Atala. I managed to guard her against the torrents of rain by placing her beneath the inclining trunk of a birch-tree, under which I sat down, holding my well-beloved upon my knees, and warming her naked feet between my hands; and thus I found myself happier than the young spouse who feels her future offspring quiver in her bosom for the first time.

"The desert now unrolled before us its immeasurable solitudes,"

"We were listening to the sound of the tempest, when all of a sudden I felt one of Atala's tears fall upon my breast. 'Storm of the heart,' I cried to myself, 'is it a drop of your rain?' Then embracing her I loved, I said, 'Atala, you are concealing something from me. Open your heart to me, O beauty! It does one so much good when a friend looks into one's soul. Tell me this secret of grief which you persist in hiding from me. Ah! I see you are weeping for your country.' She immediately retorted, 'Child of men, why should I weep for my country, since my father came not from the land of palms?' — 'What!' I replied, with profound astonishment, 'your father was not from the land of palms! What was he then who brought you upon this earth? Reply!' Atala answered in these words:

"'Before my mother brought to the warrior Simaghan, as a marriage portion, thirty mares, twenty buffaloes, a hundred measures of nut-oil, fifty beaver-skins, and a quantity of other riches, she had known a man of white flesh. Now the mother of my mother threw water in her face, and forced her to marry the magnanimous Simaghan, who was like unto a king, and honored by the people as a genius. But my mother said to her new spouse, "My bosom has conceived; kill me." Simaghan replied to her, "May the Great Spirit preserve me from such an action! I will not mutilate you. I will neither cut off your nose nor your ears, because you have been sincere and have not betrayed my couch. The fruit of your bosom shall be my fruit, and I will not visit you till after the departure of the bird of the rice-fields, when the thirteenth moon shall have shone." About that time I issued from my mother's bosom, and I began to grow, proud as a Spaniard and as a savage. My mother made me a Christian, so that her God and the God of my father might also be my God. Afterwards love-sickness fell upon her, and she went down into the little pit furnished with skins, from which no one ever comes out.'

"Such was Atala's story. 'And who was your father, then, poor orphan?' I said to her; 'how was he called by men upon earth, and what name did he bear among the genii?' — 'I never washed my father's feet,' said Atala: 'I only know that he lived with his sister at Saint Augustine, and that he ever remained faithful to my mother. Philip was his name amongst the angels, and men called him Lopez.'"

"At these words I uttered a cry which re-echoed throughout the solitude; the soumis of my transports mingled with those of the storm. Pressing Atala to my heart, I exclaimed with sobs, 'O my sister! O daughter of Lopez! daughter of my benefactor!' Atala, alarmed, sought to ascertain the cause of my agitation; but when she learnt that Lopez was the generous host who had adopted me at Saint Augustine, and whom I had quitted in order to be free, she was herself stricken with joy and confusion.

"This fraternal friendship which came upon us and joined its love to our love, was too much for our hearts. Already had I intoxicated myself with her breath, already had I drunk all the magic of love upon her lips. With my eyes raised towards heaven, amidst the flash of the lightnings, I held my spouse in my arms in the presence of the Eternal. Splendid pomp, worthy of our misfortunes and of the grandeur of our loves; superb forests, that shook your creeping plants and your leafy domes as though they were to be the curtains and the canopy of our couch; overflowing river, roaring mountains, frightful and sublime Nature, were you then but a combination prepared to deceive us, and could you not for one moment conceal a man's felicity amidst your mysterious horrors?

"Suddenly a vivid flash, followed by a clap of thunder, ran through the thickness of the shades, filled the forest with sulphur and light, and rent a tree close by us. We fled. O surprise! In the silence which followed, we heard the sound of a bell. Both speechless, we listened to the sound, so strange in a desert. At the same instant a dog barked in the distance. It approached, redoubled its cries, came up to us, and howled with joy at our feet. An old hermit, carrying a small lantern, was following the animal through the darkness of the forest. 'Heaven be praised!' he cried, as soon as he perceived us; 'I have been looking for you a long time! Our dog smelt you as soon as the storm commenced, and has guided me hither. Poor children, how young you are, and how you must have suffered! Come; I have brought a bear-skin. It shall be for this young woman, and there is some wine in our gourd. Let God be praised in all His works! His mercy is great and His goodness is infinite!'

"Atala threw herself at the feet of the monk. 'Chief of prayer,' said she to him, 'I am a Christian. Heaven has sent you to save me!' 'My daughter,' said the hermit, raising her up, 'we usually ring the mission-bell during the night and during tempests, to call strangers; and, in imitation of the example of our brethren of the Alps and of the Liban, we have taught our dog to discover lost travellers.'

"I scarcely understood the hermit. This charity appeared to me so much above man that I thought I was dreaming. By the light of the little lantern the monk was holding in his hand I saw that his beard and hair were saturated with water; his feet, his hands, and his face were bleeding: from their encounters with the brambles. 'Old man!' I at length cried, 'what sort of heart have you, that you did not fear being struck by the lightning?' 'Fear!' retorted the father, with a certain ardor, 'fear when men are in danger and I can be useful to them! I should in that case be an unworthy servant of Jesus Christ!' 'But do you know,' I interrupted, 'that I am not a Christian?' 'Young man,' replied the hermit, 'did I ask you your religion? Jesus Christ did not say, "My blood shall wash this one or that one." He died for the Jew and for the Gentile, and He only considered all the races of men as brothers in misfortune. What I am now doing for you is but little, and you would find elsewhere plenty of other help; but the glory of it should not fall upon the priests. What are we poor hermits, if not the coarse instruments of a celestial work? And what soldier would be cowardly enough to retreat when his Chief, with the cross in His hand and His forehead covered with thorns, marches before him to the assistance of suffering humanity?'

"These words went to my heart; tears of admiration and tenderness fell from my eyes. 'My dear children,' said the missionary, 'I govern in these forests a little flock of your wild brethren. My grotto is not far from here, in the mountain. Come and warm yourselves under my roof. You will not find the conveniences of life there, but you shall have shelter, and you should thank the Divine goodness even for that, for there are many men who are without it.'

"In my turn, I did all in my power to ornament her attire,"

"Like a pair of migratory swans, we traversed the solitary waves,"

II.

THE LABORERS.

There are some righteous people whose conscience is so tranquil that one cannot approach them without participating in the peace emitted, so to say, by their heart and by their language. As the hermit went on speaking, I felt the passions calm down in my bosom, and even the storm of heaven appeared to recede at his voice. The clouds were soon sufficiently dispersed to permit us to quit our retreat. We issued from the forest, and commenced climbing a high mountain. The dog walked by our side, carrying the extinguished lantern at the end of a stick.

I held Atala by the hand, and we followed the missionary. He frequently turned round to look at us, and seemed to pity our youth and our misfortunes. A book was hanging from his neck, and he leant upon a white staff. His figure was tall, his face pale and thin, and his countenance simple and sincere. His features showed that he had seen bad days, and the deep wrinkles in his forehead were the noble scars of passions overcome by virtue and by the love of God and of man. When he spoke to us standing and motionless, his long beard, his eyes modestly cast downwards, the affectionate tone of his voice, everything about him was calm and sublime. Whoever, like myself, has seen Father Aubry with his breviary and staff, on his lonely way in the desert, preserves a veritable idea of the Christian traveller upon earth.

"After half an hour's dangerous march through the paths of the mountain, we arrived at the missionary's grotto. We entered it over an accumulation of wet ivy and wild plants, washed down from the rocks by the rain. There was nothing in the place beyond a mat of papaya-leaves, a gourd for drawing up water, a few wooden vessels, a spade, a harmless serpent, and, upon a block of stone that served as a table, a crucifix and the Book of the Christians.

"The man of ancient days was not long in lighting a fire with some dried leaves. He then crushed some Indian corn between two stones, and having made a cake with it, placed it beneath the ashes to bake. When the cake had come to a fine golden color, he served it to us hot, with nut-cream, in a maple bowl. The evening having restored calm, the servant of the Great Spirit proposed that we should go and sit at the entrance to the grotto, which commanded an immense view. The remains of the storm had been carried in disorder towards the east; the fires of the conflagration caused in the forests by the lightning were still shining in the distance; at the foot of the mountain an entire pine-wood had been thrown down into the mud, and the river was charged pell-mell with molten clay, trunks of trees, and the bodies of dead animals and of dead fishes, floating upon the still agitated surface of the waters.

"It was in the midst of this scene that Atala related our history to the old genius of the mountain. His heart appeared to be touched, and tears fell upon his beard. 'My child,' he said to Atala, 'you must offer your sufferings to God, for whose glory you have already done so many things. He will give you rest. Look at those smoking forests, those receding torrents, those scattered clouds: do you imagine that He who can calm such a tempest cannot appease the troubles of the heart of man? If you have no better retreat, my dear daughter, I offer you a place amongst the flock I have had the happiness of calling to Jesus Christ. I will instruct Chactas, and I will give him to you as a husband when he shall have proved himself worthy to be your spouse.'

"At these words I fell at the hermit's knees, shedding tears of joy; but Atala became as pale as death. The old man raised me with benignity, and I then perceived that both his hands were mutilated. Atala at once comprehended his misfortunes. 'The barbarians!' she exclaimed.

"'My daughter,' replied the hermit, with a pleasant smile, 'what is that in comparison with the sufferings of my Divine Master? If the Indian idolators have tortured me, they are poor, blind creatures, whom God will enlighten some day. I love them all the more for the injury they have done me. I could not remain in my country, to which I had gone back, and where an illustrious queen did me the honor to look upon these poor marks of my apostolate. And what more glorious reward could I receive for my labors than that of obtaining, from the head of our religion, the permission to celebrate the Divine sacrifice with these mutilated hands? It only remained for me, after such an honor, to try and render myself worthy of it; so I returned to the; new world to pass the rest of my lift: in the service of my God. I have dwelt in these solitudes nearly thirty years, and it will be twenty-two to-morrow since I took possession of this rock. When I came to the place, I encountered but a few wandering families, whose manners were ferocious and whose life was miserable. I have induced them to listen to the word of Peace, and their manners have become gradually softened. They now live together at the foot of this mountain. Whilst teaching them the way of salvation, I endeavored to instruct them in the primary arts of life, but without carrying them too far, and constantly keeping the honest people within the bounds of that simplicity which constitutes happiness. Fearing to trouble them by my presence, I retired to this grotto, where they come to consult me. It is here that far from man, I admire God in the grandeur of the solitude, and prepare myself for the death which the length of my years announces to me as approaching.'

"It was in the shade of such smiling quarters, prepared by the great spirit, that we stopped to repose ourselves,"

"On finishing this discourse, the hermit fell upon his knees, and we imitated his example. He began in a loud voice a prayer to which Atala responded. Some dull flashes of lightning still opened the sky in the east, and upon the western clouds three suns seemed to be shining at the same time.

"We re-entered the grotto, where the hermit stretched out a bed of cypress-moss for Atala. Profound language was depicted in the eyes and movements of the maiden. She looked at Father Aubry as though she wished to reveal a secret to him; but something appeared to deter her from so doing—either my presence, or a sort of shame, or perhaps the uselessness of the avowal. I heard her get up in the middle of the night. She went to look for the hermit; but, as he had given up his couch to Atala, he had gone to contemplate the beauty of the heavens, and to pray to God on the top of the mountain. He told me the next day that such was his custom, even during winter, as he loved to see the forests wave their stripped summits, the clouds fly through the air, and to hear the winds and the torrents roar in the solitude. My sister was therefore obliged to return to her couch, where she immediately fell asleep. Alas! full of hope, I thought Atala's weakness was nothing more than a passing sign of weariness.

"The following morning I was awakened by the songs of the cardinals and the mockingbirds, nestled in the acacias and laurels that surrounded the grotto. I went forth and gathered a magnolia rose, and placed it, wet with the tears of the morning, upon the head of my sleeping Atala. I hoped, according to the religion of my country, that the soul of some child dead at the breast might have descended upon this flower in a dew-drop, and that a happy dream might convey it to the bosom of my future spouse. I afterwards sought my host. I found him, his gown turned up into his two pockets, and a chaplet in his hand, waiting for me, seated upon the trunk of a pine-tree that had fallen from old age. He proposed that we should go together to the Mission while Atala was still reposing. I accepted his offer, and we immediately started on our way.

"On descending the mountain, I perceived some oaks upon which the genii seemed to have drawn foreign characters. The hermit told me that he had traced them himself; that they were some verses of an ancient poet called Homer, and a few sentences of another poet, more ancient still, named Solomon. There was a sort of mysterious harmony between the wisdom of former times, the verses eaten into by moss, the old hermit who had engraved them, and the aged oaks which had served him for books.

"His name, his age, and the date of his mission were also marked upon a reed of the savannah at the foot of those trees. I was surprised at the fragility of the latter monument. 'It will last longer than I,' replied the father, 'and it will always be of more value than the little good I have done.'

"From thence we arrived at the entrance to a valley, where I saw a wonderful work. It was a natural bridge, similar to that in Virginia, of which you have perhaps heard. Men, my son, especially those of your country, often imitate Nature, and their copies are always insignificant. It is not the same with Nature when she appears to imitate the labors of men by in reality offering them models. Then it is that she throws bridges from the summit of one mountain to the summit of another, suspends roads in the air, spreads rivers for canals, carves out hills for columns, and for basins excavates seas.

"We passed beneath the sole arch of this bridge, and found ourselves in front of another wonder, the cemetery of the Indians of the Mission, or the Groves of Death. Father Aubry had permitted his neophytes to bury their dead in their manner, and to continue its original name to their place of sepulture. He had merely sanctified the place with a cross.[11] The soil was divided, like fields set out for harvest, into as many lots as there were families. Each lot formed a wood of itself, which varied according to the taste of those who had planted it. A stream meandered noiselessly through the groves. It went by the name of the River of Peace. This smiling refuge of souls was closed on the east by the bridge beneath which we had passed. Two hills bounded it on the north and on the south, and it was open only towards the west, where stood a large forest of fir trees. The trunks of these trees, spotted with green, and growing without branches up to their very summits, resembled tall columns, and formed the peristyle of this temple of death. We remarked a religious sound, similar to the half-suppressed murmurs of an organ beneath the roof of a church; but when we had penetrated into the interior of the sanctuary, we could hear nothing beyond the hymns of the birds celebrating an eternal fête to the memory of the dead.

"On emerging from the wood, we perceived the village of the Mission, situated on the side of a lake, in the midst of a savannah planted with flowers. It was reached by an avenue of magnolias and oaks, which bordered one of 'those ancient roads met with towards the mountains that separate Kentucky from the Floridas. As soon as the Indians saw their pastor in the plain, they abandoned their labors, and hastened to meet him. Some of them kissed his gown, others assisted him to walk; the mothers raised their little children in their arms to show them the man of Jesus Christ who had shed tears. Father Aubry inquired as he went along of what was going on in the village. He gave counsel to one, and a mild reprimand to another, He spoke of harvests to be gathered, of children to be instructed, of troubles to be consoled; and he alluded to God in every topic he touched upon.

"Thus escorted, we arrived at the foot of the large cross placed by the roadside. It was here that the servant of God was in the habit of celebrating the mysteries of his religion. 'My dear neophytes,' said he, turning himself towards the crowd, 'a brother and a sister have come up to you, and, as an additional happiness, I see that Providence spared your harvests yesterday. Behold two great reasons for thankfulness. Let us therefore offer up the holy sacrifice, and may each of you bring to it deep attention, a lively faith, infinite gratitude, and a humble heart!'

"The holy priest forthwith put on a white tunic of mulberry-bark; the sacred cups were withdrawn from a tabernacle at the foot of the cross; the altar was set out on a portion of the rock, water was procured from the neighboring torrent, and a bunch of wild grapes furnished the wine for the sacrifice. We all went down upon our knees in the high grass, and the mystery began.

---

[11] Father Aubry had done like the Jesuits in China, who allowed the Chinese to inter their relations in their gardens, according to an ancient custom.

"Break of day, appearing from behind the mountains, inflamed the eastern sky. Everything in the solitude was golden or roseate. The sun, announced by so much splendor, at length issued from an abyss of light, and its first ray fell upon the consecrated host, which the priest was at that very moment raising in the air.

"After the sacrifice, during which nothing was wanting to me but the daughter of Lopez, we went to the village. The most touching mixture of social and natural life reigned there. By the side of a cypress-wood of the ancient desert was a nascent vegetation; ears of corn rolled like gold about the trunk of a fallen oak, and summer sheaves replaced the tree of three centuries. On all sides forests given up to the flames were sending up their smoke into the air, and the plough was being pushed slowly through the remains of their roots. Surveyors with long chains went to measure the ground; arbitrators marked out the first properties; the bird gave up its nest; the den of the wild beast was converted into a cabin; forges were heard to roar, and the blows of the axe caused the echoes to resound for the last time as they expired with the trees which had served them for a refuse.

"I wandered with delight in the midst of these scenes, rendered still more enchanting by the image of Atala and by the dreams of felicity with which I was feeding my heart. I admired the triumph of Christianity over savage life. I saw the Indian becoming civilized by the voice of religion; I assisted at the primitive union of man and the earth—man, by this great contract, abandoning to the earth the inheritance of his labors; and the earth undertaking in return to bear faithfully the harvests, the sons, and the ashes of man.

"During this time a child was presented to the missionary, who baptized it among the flowering jessamine on the border of a spring, whilst a coffin, in the midst of these joys and labors, was being carried to the Groves of Death. Two spouses received the nuptial benediction beneath an oak, and we afterwards went to install them in a corner of the desert. The pastor walked in front of us, blessing here and there a rock, a tree or a fountain, as of old, according to the book of the Christians, God blessed the untilled land when He gave it to Adam for an inheritance. This procession, which, with the flocks, was following its venerable chief from rock to rock, represented to my affected heart the migrations of the first families, when Shem, with his children, advanced into an unknown world, following the sun as his guide.

"I desired to know from the hermit how he governed his flock. With great patience he replied to me, 'I have laid down no law for them; I have merely taught them to love one another, to pray to God, and to hope for a better life. All the laws in the world are comprised therein. Towards the middle of the village you may perceive a cabin somewhat larger than the rest. It serves as a chapel during the rainy season. My children assemble there morning and evening to praise the Lord, and when I am absent an old man offers up the prayers; for old age, like maternity, is a sort of priesthood. The people afterwards go to work in the fields; and although the properties are divided, in order that each may learn something of social economy, the harvests are deposited in the same storehouse, out of a spirit of brotherly charity. Four old men are charged with the equal distribution of the produce of the general labors. Add to all that our religious ceremonies, plenty of hymns, the cross where I celebrate the mysteries, the elm-tree beneath which I preach in fine weather, our tombs near our corn-fields, our rivers into which I plunge the little children, and the Saint Johns of this new Bethany, and you will have a complete idea of this kingdom of Jesus Christ.'

"The language of the hermit delighted me, and I felt the superiority of this stable and busy life over the wandering and idle existence of the savage.

"Ah, René! I do not repine against Providence, yet I confess I never think of that evangelical society without experiencing bitter regret. How a hut, with Atala, in that neighborhood, would have rendered my life happy! There all my wanderings would have ceased; there, with a spouse, ignored by men and concealing my happiness in the depths of the forest, my days would have flown by like those rivers which have not even a name in the desert. Instead of the peace I was then bold enough to promise myself, amidst what troubles have my years been cast! The constant plaything of fortune, wrecked upon every shore, long an exile from my country, and on my return thither finding only a ruined cabin and friends in the tomb—such was to be the destiny of Chactas.

"Every evening we lighted a large fire and built a travelling hut,"

III.

THE DRAMA.

If my dream of happiness was bright, it was also of short duration, and I was to be awakened from it at the hermit's grotto. On arriving there in the middle of the clay, I was surprised at not seeing Atala come forth to meet us. I cannot tell what sudden apprehension took possession of me. As we approached the grotto, I dared not call the daughter of Lopez; my imagination was equally frightened by the idea of the noise or of the silence that might follow my cries. Still more terrified by the dark appearance of the entrance to the rock, I said to the missionary, 'O you, whom heaven accompanies and strengthens, penetrate into those shades!'

"How weak is the man who is governed by his passions! How strong is he who relies upon God! There was more courage in that religious heart, withered by seventy-six years, than in all the ardor of my youth. The man of peace entered the grotto, whilst I remained outside, full of terror. Soon a feeble murmur of complaint issued from the interior of the rock, and fell upon my ear. Uttering a cry as I recovered my strength, I rushed into the darkness of the cavern. Spirits of my fathers, you alone know the spectacle that met my view!

"The hermit had lighted a pine-torch, which he was holding with a trembling hand over Atala's couch. With her hair in disorder, the young and beautiful woman, slightly raised upon her elbow, looked pale and suffering. Drops of painful sweat shone upon her forehead; her half-extinguished eyes still sought to express her love to me, and her mouth endeavored to smile. As though struck by lightning, with my eyes fixed, my arms outstretched, and my lips apart, I remained motionless. A profound silence reigned for a moment between the three personages of this scene of grief. The hermit was the first to break it. 'This,' he said, 'can only be a fever occasioned by fatigue, and if we resign ourselves to God's will, He will take pity on us.'

"At these words my heart revived, and, with the mobility of the savage, I passed suddenly from an excess of fear to an excess of confidence, from which, however, Atala soon aroused me. Shaking her head sadly, she made us a sign to approach her couch.

"'My father,' she said, in a weak voice, addressing herself to the hermit, 'I am upon the point of death. O Chactas! listen without despair to the fatal secret I had concealed from you in order not to make you too miserable, and out of obedience to my mother. Try not to interrupt me by any marks of grief, which would shorten the few moments I have to live. I have many things to tell of, and from the beatings of my heart, which slacken—I do not know what icy burden presses within my bosom—I feel that I cannot make too much haste!'

"After a short silence, Atala continued thus:—

"'My sad destiny began almost before I had seen the light. My mother had conceived me in misfortune. I wearied her bosom, and she brought me into the world with such painful difficulty that my life was despaired of. To save me, my mother made a vow. She promised the Queen of Angels that I should consecrate myself to an unwedded life if I escaped from death. That fatal vow is now hurrying me to the tomb!

"'I was entering upon my sixteenth year when I lost my mother. Some hours before her death she called me to her bedside. "My daughter," she said, in the presence of the missionary who was consoling her last moments, "you know the vow I made for you. Would you belie your mother? O my Atala, I am leaving you in a world that is not worthy of possessing a Christian—in the midst of idolators who persecute the God of your father and of your mother, the God who, after having given you life, has preserved it to you by a miracle. Ah, my dear child, by accepting the virgin's veil, you only renounce the cares of the cabin and the fatal passions which have tormented your mother's breast! Come, then, my well-beloved, come; swear upon this image of the Saviour's Mother, held by the hands of this holy priest and of your dying parent, that you will not betray me in the face of heaven. Remember what I promised for you in order to save your life, and that, if you do not keep my promise, you will plunge your mother's soul into eternal tortures."

"'O my mother, why spake you thus? O Religion, the cause of my ills and of my felicity, my ruin and my consolation at the same time! And you, dear and sad object of a passion that is consuming me even in the arms of death, you can now see, O Chactas, what has caused the hardship of our destiny! Melting into tears, and throwing myself upon my mother's bosom, I promised all that I was asked to promise. The missionary pronounced over me the fearful language of my oath, and gave me the scapulary that bound me forever. My mother threatened me with her malediction if ever I broke my vow; and, after having advised me to keep the secret inviolably from the pagans, the persecutors of my religion, she expired, whilst holding me in a tender embrace.

"The great spirit knows that at this moment I saw and thought of nothing but Atala,"

"The forests bent; the sky opened time after time, and from between the interstices other skies and ardent scenes might be perceived,"

"The conflagration extended like a head-dress of flame,"

"He had gone to contemplate the beauty of the heavens, and to pray to god on the top of the mountain,"

"'I did not at first know the danger of my oath. Full of ardor and a veritable Christian, proud, too, of the Spanish blood that flowed in my veins, I saw myself surrounded by men unworthy of receiving my hand, and I congratulated myself upon having no other spouse than the God of my mother. I saw you, young and beautiful prisoner; I pitied your lot; I had the courage to speak to you at the funeral pile in the forest. Then it was that I felt the weight of my vows!'

"When Atala had finished littering these words, I cried out, with clenched fists, and looking at the missionary with a threatening air, 'This, then, is the religion you have so much vaunted to me! Perish the oath that deprives me of Atala! Man-priest, why did you come into these forests?'

'"To save you,' said the old man, in a terrible voice; 'to conquer your passions, and to prevent you, blasphemer, from drawing down upon yourself the wrath of Heaven! It is becoming, indeed, for so young a man, scarcely entered upon life, to complain of his griefs! Where are the marks of your sufferings? Where are the acts of injustice you have had to support? Where are your virtues, which alone could give you a certain right to murmur? What services have you rendered? What good have you done? What, miserable creature! you can only show me passions, and you dare to accuse Heaven! When, like Father Aubry, you shall have passed thirty years in exile upon the mountains, you will be less prompt to judge of the designs of Providence. You will then understand that you know nothing and are nothing, and that there is no chastisement so severe, no misfortune so terrible, that our corrupt flesh does not deserve to suffer.'

"The lightnings that flashed from the old man's eyes, the beatings of his beard against his breast, and his fiery language, made him like to a god. Overcome by his majesty, I fell at the father's knees, and asked pardon for my anger. 'My son,' he replied, in a tone so mild that a feeling of remorse entered my soul, 'it was not for myself that I reprimanded you. Alas! you are right, my dear child: I have done but very little in these forests, and God has no servant more unworthy than myself. But, my son, it is Heaven—Heaven, I say—that should never be accused! Pardon me if I have offended you, and let us listen to your sister. There may still perhaps be some remedy; do not let us tire of hoping. Chactas, the religion which has made a virtue of hope is a Divine religion!'

"'My young friend,' resumed Atala, 'you have been a witness of my struggles, and nevertheless you have seen but the smallest portion of them. I concealed the rest from you. No; the black slave who moistens the hot sands of the Floridas with his sweat is less miserable than Atala has been. Urging you to flight, and yet certain to die if you left me; fearful of flying with you to the desert, and still panting after the shade of the woods—ah! if it had only been required of me to abandon my relations, my friends, my country! if even (frightful thought!) I should only have incurred the loss of my soul! But thy shadow, O my mother! thy shadow was always there, reminding me of thy tortures! I heard thy complaints; I saw the flames of hell consuming thee. My nights were barren, and haunted by phantoms, my days were disconsolate; the evening dew dried as it fell upon my burning skin; I opened my lips to the breezes, and the breezes, far from refreshing me, became heated with the fire of my breath. What torture it was for me, Chactas, to see you constantly near me, far from all mankind, in the depths of the solitude, and to feel that there was an invincible barrier between you and myself! To have passed my life at your feet, to have waited upon you like a slave, to have prepared your repasts and your couch in some unknown corner of the universe, would have been for me supreme happiness. That happiness was within my reach, yet I could not enjoy it. What plans I have imagined! What dreams have passed through this sad heart of mine! Occasionally, when I fixed my eyes upon you, I went so far as to encourage desires that were as foolish as they were culpable: sometimes I wished I were the only creature living with you upon the earth: at other times, feeling a divinity that stopped me in my horrible transports, I seemed to desire that that divinity might be annihilated, provided that, pressed in your arms, I might roll from abyss to abyss with the ruins of God and of the world! Even now—shall I say it?—now that eternity is about to swallow me up, that I am going to appear before the inexorable Judge; at the moment when, from obedience to my mother, I see with joy my vow devouring my life; well, even now, by a frightful contradiction, I carry away with me the regret of not having been yours——'

"'My daughter,' interrupted the missionary, 'your grief misleads you. The excess of passion to which you are abandoning yourself is rarely just; it is not even natural; and for that reason it is less culpable in the eyes of God, because it is rather an error of the mind than a vice of the heart. You must therefore put away such passionate feelings, which are unworthy of your innocence. At the same time, my dear child; your impetuous imagination has alarmed you too much concerning your vows. Religion requires no superhuman sacrifice. Its true sentiments, its moderated virtues, are far above the exalted sentiments and the forced virtues of a pretending heroism. If you had succumbed—well, poor lost sheep! the Good Shepherd would have sought for you, and would have brought you back to the flock. The treasures of repentance were open to you; torrents of blood are required to wipe out our faults in the eyes of men; a single tear suffices with God. Tranquilize yourself, therefore, my dear daughter; your situation needs calm. Let us address ourselves to God, who heals all the wounds of His servants. If it be His will, as I trust it may be, that you escape from this malady, I will write to the Bishop of Quebec; he has the power to release you from your vows, which are but simple vows; and you shall finish your days near me, with Chactas as your spouse.'

"As the old man finished speaking, Atala was seized with a violent convulsion, from which she emerged with all the signs of fearful suffering. 'What!' said she, joining her two hands with passion, 'there was a remedy! I could have been released from my vows!' 'Yes, my daughter,' replied the father; 'and it is still time.' 'It is too late it is too late!' she cried.

'Must I die at the moment when I learn that I might have been happy? Why did I not know, this old man sooner? At present what happiness should I be enjoying with you, with my Chactas, a Christian—consoled, comforted by this august priest—in this desert—for ever—Oh! my felicity would have been too great!' 'Calm yourself,' I said to her, taking hold of one of the unfortunate maiden's hands; 'calm yourself: that happiness is still in store for us.' 'Never! never!' said Atala. 'How?' I asked. 'You do not know all,' cried the maiden. 'Yesterday—during the storm—I was on the point of breaking my vows; I was going to plunge my mother into the flames of the abyss. Already her malediction was upon me, already I lied to the God who had saved my life. Whilst you were kissing my trembling lips, you were not aware that you were embracing death!' 'O heaven!' cried the missionary; 'dear child, what have you done?' 'A crime, my father,' said Atala, with her eyes wandering; 'but I only destroyed myself, and I saved my mother.' 'Finish then!' I exclaimed, full of fear. 'Well,' she said, 'I had foreseen my weakness; and on quitting the cabins I took away with me— —'

'What?' I interrupted with horror. 'A poison?' said the father. 'It is now at my heart,' cried Atala.

"The torch slipped from the hermit's hand. I fell fainting near Lopez's daughter. The old man took each of us in his arms, and during a short interval we all three mingled our sobs on the funeral couch.

"'Let us be stirring; let us be stirring,' said the courageous father, as he rose to light a lamp. 'We are losing precious moments: like intrepid Christians, let us brave the assaults of adversity; with the cord about our necks, and with ashes upon our heads, let us throw ourselves at the feet of the Most High, to implore His clemency, and to submit ourselves to His decrees. Perhaps it may still be time. My daughter, you ought to have told me of this last night.'

"'Alas! my father,' said Atala, 'I looked for you last night; but heaven, as a punishment for my faults, kept you away from me. Besides, all help would have been useless; for even the Indians themselves, who are so clever in what concerns poisons, know no remedy for that I have taken. O Chactas, judge of my astonishment when I found that the result was not so prompt as I had expected! My love redoubled my strength, and my soul was unwilling to separate thus quickly from you!'

"It was no longer by sobs that I now interrupted Atala's recital, but by a torrent of passionate transports known only to savages. I rolled myself upon the ground, twisting my arms and biting my hands. The old priest, with wonderful tenderness, ran from brother to sister, endeavoring to relieve us in a thousand ways. Through the calmness of his heartland from the experience due to his weight of years, he knew how to act upon our youth, and his religion furnished him with accents even more tender and more ardent than our passions. Does not this priest, who had passed forty years of daily sacrifice in the service of God and man upon the mountain, remind you of the holocausts of Israel smoking perpetually on the high places before the Lord?

"Alas! it was in vain that he tried to procure a remedy for Atala's sufferings. Fatigue, grief, poison, and a passion more mortal than all the poisons together, had united to snatch the flower from the desert. Towards evening terrible symptoms began to show themselves. A general numbness took possession of Atala's limbs, and the extremities of her body became cold. 'Touch my fingers,' she said to me; 'do they not feel quite icy?' I could not reply. I was overcome with horror. Afterwards she added, 'Even yesterday, my well-beloved, your contact made me quiver: and now I can no longer feel your hand; I scarcely hear your voice, and the objects in the grotto are disappearing from my sight one after the other. Are not the birds singing? The sun must be nearly setting? Chactas, its rays will be very beautiful in the desert, over my tomb!'

"Atala perceiving that her language had melted us into tears, said softly, 'Pardon me, my kind friends; I am very weak, but perhaps I shall get stronger. And yet to die so young, all at once, when my heart was so full of life! Chief of prayer, take pity on me; support me. Do you think my mother will be satisfied, and that God will forgive what I have done?'

"'My daughter,' replied the holy man, shedding tears, and wiping them away with his trembling, mutilated fingers, 'all your misfortunes are the result of your ignorance. Your savage education and the want of instruction have been your ruin. You did not know that a Christian cannot dispose of his life. Console yourself, therefore, my dear lamb; God will pardon you, on account of the simplicity of your heart. Your mother, and the imprudent missionary who guided her, are more to be blamed than you; they exceeded their power in imposing an indiscreet vow upon you: but may the Lord be with them! You all three offer a terrible example of the dangers of enthusiasm, and of the want of enlightenment on religious matters. Be of good cheer, my child; He who fathoms our thoughts and our hearts will judge you according to your intentions, which were pure, and not from your action, which was condemnable.

"'As for life, if the moment has come for you to sleep in the Lord, ah! my child, you lose but little by losing this world! In spite of the solitude in which you have lived, you have known sorrow; what would you have felt, then, if you had witnessed the evils of society?—if, on visiting the shores of Europe, your ear had been stricken by the long cry of suffering heard throughout that old land? The dweller in the cabin, the inhabitant of a palace, both suffer and groan here below: queens have been seen to cry like simple women, and people have been astonished at the quantity of tears shed by kings!

"'Is it your love that you regret? My daughter, you might as well weep over a dream. Do you know the heart of man, and could you reckon upon the inconstancies of his affection? Sacrifices and kindnesses, Atala, are not eternal ties. One day, perhaps, disgust would have come with satiety, the past would have been considered as nothing, and naught would have remained but the inconveniences of a poor and despised union. Doubtless, my dear daughter, the most beautiful loves were those of the man and woman who issued from the hand of the Creator. A paradise had been prepared for them. They were innocent and immortal. Perfect in soul and body, they suited each other in every respect. Eve had been created for Adam, 1 and Adam for Eve. If they, nevertheless, could not remain in that state of happiness, what couple after them could do so? I will not speak to you of the marriages of the first-born of men, of those ineffable unions between sister and brother, in which love and friendship were confounded in the same heart, and the purity of the one increased the delights of the other. All those unions were troubled; jealousy crept over the altar of turf upon which the goat was sacrificed, it existed beneath the tent of Abraham, and even in the abodes of the patriarchs, where they experienced so much joy that they forgot the death of their mothers.

"We remarked a religious sound, similar to the half-suppressed murmurs of an organ beneath the roof of a church,"

"'Do you suppose, then, my child, that you are more innocent and more fortunate in your ties than those holy families from which Jesus Christ deigned to descend? Again, woman renews her sufferings each time she becomes a mother, and she weeps on her marriage-day. What grief there is for her in the mere loss of her new-born babe, to whom she gave nourishment, and who dies upon her bosom! The mountain was full of groans: nothing could console Rachel for the loss of her sons. The bitterness attendant upon human affections is so powerful that I have in my country seen grand ladies, the beloved of kings, quit the life of a court to bury themselves in a cloister, and mutilate that rebellious flesh, the pleasures of which are only the precursors of sorrow.

"'But perhaps you would say that these last examples do not affect you; that all your ambition was limited to the desire of living in an obscure cabin with the man of your choice; that you sought less after the sweets of marriage than after the charms of that folly which youth calls love? Delusion, chimera, vanity—the dream of a diseased imagination! I also, my daughter, have known the troubles of the heart. This head has not been always bald, nor this breast always so calm as it appears to you to-day. Believe in my experience: if man, constant in his affections, could unceasingly respond to a sentiment constantly renewed, solitude and love would doubtless render him the equal of God Himself; for those are the two eternal pleasures of the Great Being. But the soul of man becomes weary, and never loves the same object long and fully. There are always some points upon which two hearts do not agree, and in the end those points suffice to render life insupportable.

"'Finally, my dear child, the great error of men, in their dream of happiness, is that they forget the infirmity of death inseparable from their nature; the end must come. Sooner or later, whatever might have been your felicity, your beautiful visage would have been changed into that uniform face which the sepulchre gives to the family of Adam. Even the eye of Chactas would not have been able to distinguish you from amongst your sisters of the tomb. Love does not extend its empire so far as the worms in the coffin. What have I to say (O vanity of vanities!), what can I say concerning the durability of earthly friendships? Would you, my dear daughter, know its extent? If a man were to return to light some years after his death, I do not believe he would be received with joy even by those who had shed the most tears to his memory; so quickly are new ties contracted, so easily fresh habits are indulged in, so entirely is inconstancy natural to man, and so little is our life even in the hearts of our friends!

"'Thank, therefore, the Divine goodness, my dear daughter, for taking you away thus early from this valley of misery. Already the white robe and the brilliant crown of virgins are being prepared for you in the skies; already I hear the Queen of the Angels crying out to you, "Come, my worthy servant; come, my dove; come and sit down upon the throne of candor, amidst all those maidens who have sacrificed their beauty and their youth in the service of humanity, in the education of children, and in works of penitence."'

"As the last ray of daylight stills the winds and spreads tranquillity through the sky, so the old man's calm language appeased the passions in the bosom of my lover. She no longer thought of anything but my grief, and of the means for enabling me to support her loss. At first she said that she should die happy if I would promise her to dry my tears; then she spoke to me of my mother and of my country, and endeavored to distract me from present grief by referring to past sufferings. She exhorted me to patience and virtue. 'You will not always be unhappy,' she said; 'if Heaven tries you to-day, it is merely to render you more compassionate for the ills of others. The heart, Chactas, is like those trees that only yield their balm for healing men's wounds after having been themselves seared with iron.'

"When she had thus spoken, Atala turned towards the missionary, seeking from him the consolation she had been endeavoring to impart to me; and, by turns consoling and consoled, she gave and received the word of life; upon the couch of death.

"Nevertheless, the hermit redoubled his zeal. With the torch of religion in his hand, he appeared to be guiding Atala to the tomb, to show her its secret wonders. The humble grotto was full of the grandeur of this Christian agony, and the heavenly spirits were no doubt attentive to the scene, in which Religion had to struggle alone against Love, Youth and Death.

"Divine Religion triumphed, and her victory was perceptible from the holy sadness that followed our hearts' previous passionate transports. Towards the middle of the night, Atala seemed to revive, and repeated the prayers pronounced by the monk at the side of her couch. Shortly afterwards, she offered me her hand, and, in a voice scarcely audible, said, 'Son of Outalissi, do you remember the night when you took me for the Virgin of the Last Loves? What a singular omen of our destiny! She stopped, then continued: 'When I think that I am leaving you for ever, my heart makes such an effort to live, that I feel almost strong enough to render myself immortal by the power of my love. But, O God! Thy will be done!' Atala became silent during a few instants; then she added: 'It only remains for me to ask your pardon for all the ills I have caused you. Chactas, a little earth thrown upon my body will place a world between you and me, and will deliver you forever from the weight of my calamities!'

"'Pardon you!' I exclaimed, drowned in tears; 'Is it not I who have caused all your misfortunes?' 'My friend,' she replied, interrupting me, 'you have rendered me very happy, and if I had to begin my life over again, I should still prefer the happiness of having loved you for a few short moments in an exile of adversity to an entire life of repose in my own country.'

"He alluded to god in every topic he touched upon, "

"Here Atala's voice languished: the shadows of death spread themselves about her eyes and her mouth; her wandering fingers endeavored to catch at something and she spoke lowly with the invisible spirits. Soon, however, making an effort, she attempted, but in vain, to take the little crucifix from her neck; she asked me to untie it myself, and then said to me:—

"The moon lent her pale light to this funereal watching,"

"'When I spoke to you for the first time, by the light of the fire you saw this cross shining upon my bosom; it is the only treasure that Atala possesses. Lopez, your father and mine, sent it to my mother a few days after my birth. Accept the inheritance, then, from me, my brother, and keep it in remembrance of my misfortunes. Chactas, I have a last request to make of you. Our union on earth, my friend, would have been short; but after this life there is a longer life. I only go before you to-day, and I will wait for you in the celestial empire. If you have loved me, get yourself instructed in the Christian religion, which will prepare our re-union. That religion has worked a great miracle under your own eyes, since it enables me to quit you without the anguish of despair. Still, Chactas, I only desire you to make me a simple promise. I know too well what it costs to ask an oath from you. Perhaps such a vow might separate you from some woman happier than I. O my mother, pardon thy daughter! I am again succumbing to my weaknesses, and am turning aside from Thee, O my God, thoughts that should be thine, and thine only!'

"Overwhelmed with grief, I promised Atala that I would one day embrace the Christian religion. At this moment the hermit, rising with an inspired air, and stretching his arms towards the roof of the grotto, exclaimed, 'It is time—it is time to call God hither!'

"Scarcely had he uttered those words, when a supernatural force constrained me to fall upon my knees and to turn my head towards the foot of Atala's couch. The priest opened a secret place that contained a golden urn covered with a silk veil; he then knelt down and prayed fervently. Suddenly the grotto appeared to be illuminated: songs of angels and the vibrations of celestial harps were heard in the air; and when the hermit drew the sacred vessel from the tabernacle, I thought I saw God Himself issue forth from the side of the mountain.

"The priest opened the cup, took between his fingers a wafer white as snow, and approached Atala as he pronounced some mysterious words. That saint's eyes were upturned in ecstacy. All her sufferings appeared to be suspended; her entire being concentrated itself upon her mouth; her lips parted, and advanced with respect to seek the God concealed beneath the mystic bread. The saintly old man afterwards soaked a piece of cotton in the consecrated oil, and looked for a moment at the dying maiden; when all of a sudden he uttered these imposing words, 'Go, Christian soul, go; return to your Creator!' Raising then my downcast head, I cried, looking at the vessel that contained the holy oil, 'My father, will that remedy restore Atala to life?' 'Yes, my son,' said the old man, falling into my arms, 'to life eternal!' Atala had just expired.

At this point Chactas was obliged, for the second time, to interrupt the recital of his story. His tears flowed copiously, and the tremor of his voice only permitted him to utter broken words. The blind sachem opened his breast and drew forth Atala's crucifix. "Here it is!" he cried; "dear token of adversity! O René, O my son! You see it; but I can see it no longer.

Tell me whether, after so many years, the gold of it is tarnished? Do you see any traces of my tears upon it? Could you recognize the part which had been touched by the lips of a saint? How is it that Chactas is not yet a Christian? What trivial motives of policy or nationality have kept him in the errors of his fathers? No; I will no longer delay. The earth is crying out to me, 'When, then, wilt thou go down into the tomb, and for what art thou waiting to embrace a Divine religion?'.... Earth! thou shalt not wait long, for as soon as a priest shall have regenerated by baptism this head whitened with grief, I hope to be re-united to Atala.... But let me finish what remains to be told of my story."

"I took the body on my shoulders; the hermit walked in front of me, carrying a
spade in his hand,"

"Bending beneath the burden, I was obliged to lay it down often upon the moss, and sit awhile to recover my strength,"

"At length we arrived at the spot selected by my grief,"

IV.

THE FUNERAL

"I will not undertake, René, to picture the despair that took possession of my soul when Atala had heaved her last sigh. It would require more warmth than I have left, and that my closed eyes might re-open to the sun, to ask it to tell of the tears they shed in its light. Yes, the moon now shining above our heads will become weary of lighting the solitudes of Kentucky—the river that is now bearing our pirogues will suspend the course of its waters—before my tears cease to flow for Atala! During two days I was insensible to the hermit's conversation. In trying to calm my grief, the excellent man did not employ the commonplace reasonings of earthly minds. All he said was, 'My son, it is the will of God;' and then he pressed me in his arms. I should never have thought there was so much consolation in those few words of a resigned Christian, if I had not myself experienced it.

"The mild tenderness and the unvarying patience of the old servant of God at length conquered the obstinacy of my grief; I became ashamed of the tears I caused him to shed. 'My father,' I said, 'this is too much: let the passions of a young man disturb the peace of your days no longer. Permit me to carry away the remains of my spouse; I will inter them in some corner of the desert; and if I am condemned to live on for a time, I will endeavor to render myself worthy of the eternal nuptials that were promised me by Atala.'

"At this unexpected return of courage, the good father trembled with joy, saying, 'O blood of Jesus Christ, blood of my Divine Master, I acknowledge herein Thy merits! Thou wilt no doubt save this young man. My God, finish Thy work; restore peace to this troubled soul, and leave it but the humble and useful remembrances of its misfortunes!'

"The righteous man refused to give up to me the body of Lopez's daughter; but he proposed to call together his neophytes, and to inter it with all the pomp of the Christian ceremonial. In my turn, I refused. 'Atala's misfortunes and virtues,' I said, 'were unknown to men; let her grave, dug secretly by our hands, share that obscurity.' We agreed to set off the next morning at sunrise, and to bury Atala beneath the arch of the natural bridge at the entrance to the Groves of Death. It was also decided that we should pass the night in prayer near the corpse of the saint.

"Towards evening we transported the precious remains to an opening of the grotto looking to the north. The hermit had enveloped them in a piece of European lawn, woven by his mother. It was the only thing still remaining to him of his country, and he had long preserved it for his own tomb. We laid Atala upon a turf of mountain-sensitives; her feet, her head, her shoulders, and a part of her bosom were uncovered. There was a faded magnolia in her hair, the same flower I had placed upon the virgin's couch to render her fruitful. Her lips, like a rose-bud gathered two mornings before, seemed to languish and smile. Her cheeks, of sparkling whiteness, showed a number of blue veins. Her beautiful eyes were closed, her modest feet joined together, and her hands of alabaster pressed against her heart an ebony crucifix; the scapulary of her vows was fastened about her neck. She appeared as though enchanted by the angel of melancholy, and by the double sleep of innocence and of the tomb.

I never saw anything so heavenly. By a person unconscious that this young girl had enjoyed the light, she might have been taken for a statue of Sleeping Virginity.

"The monk did not cease praying all night. I sat in silence at the end of my Atala's funeral couch. How often, during her sleep, I had held that charming head upon my knees! How many times I had leaned over her to hear her breathe, and to inhale her breath! But at present no sound issued from that motionless breast, and it was in vain that I looked for the awakening of my love!

"The moon lent her pale light to this funereal watching; she rose in the middle of the night, like a white vestal come to weep over the coffin of a companion. From time to time the monk dipped a flowering branch into the holy water, and shaking its moistened leaves, perfumed the night air with heavenly balms. Occasionally also he repeated, to an ancient tune, these verses by an old poet named Job:

"Three times I evoked the soul of Atala; three times the genius of the desert responded to my cries beneath the funeral arch,"

"'I have passed away like a flower; I have withered like the grass of the fields.

"'Wherefore is light given to him that is in misery, and life unto the bitter in soul?'

"Thus sang the old man. His deep and irregular voice went rolling through the silence of the desert. The name of God and of the tomb issued from all the echoes, from all the torrents, and from all the forests, and the Groves of Death seemed to be murmuring a distant chorus of the departed in reply to the hermit's sacred chant.

"Nevertheless, a bar of gold was forming in the east. The sparrow-hawks were crying upon the rocks, and the martins creeping back into the hollows of the elm-trees: these were so many signs that the time had come for Atala's interment. I took the body on my shoulders; the hermit walked in front of me, carrying a spade in his hand. We commenced the descent from rock to rock; old age and death combined equally to slacken our pace. At the sight of the dog which had found us in the forest, and which now, jumping with joy, led us by another route, I melted into tears. Atala's long hair, the plaything of the morning breezes, frequently threw its golden veil over my eyes, and, bending beneath the burden, I was obliged to lay it down often upon the moss, and sit awhile, to recover my strength. At length we arrived at the spot selected by my grief, and we entered beneath the arch of the bridge. O my son, you should have seen the youthful savage and the old hermit, on their knees in front of each other, in the desert, digging with their hands a grave for the poor girl whose body lay stretched out close at hand, in the dried-up bed of a torrent!

"When our work was terminated, we transported the loved one into her bed of clay. Taking then a little dust in my hand, and observing a fearful silence, I looked upon Atala's face for the last time. I afterwards spread the earth over that forehead of eighteen springs; gradually I saw the features of my sister disappear, and her graces become hidden beneath the curtain of eternity. 'Lopez!' I exclaimed, 'behold your son burying your daughter!' And I finished by covering Atala entirely with the earth of sleep.

"We returned to the grotto, where I made the missionary acquainted with the project I had formed of remaining with him. The saint, who wonderfully understood the heart of man, penetrated my thought and the artfulness of my grief. He said: 'Chactas, son of Outalissi, so long as Atala was alive, I myself desired that you should live with me; but at present your lot is changed; you owe yourself to your country. Believe me, my son, such griefs are not eternal. Sooner or later they wear themselves out, because the heart of man is finite. That is one of our great miseries; we are not even capable of being unhappy for a long time. Return to the Mississippi; go and console your mother, who weeps for you day by day, and who stands in need of your support. Get yourself instructed in Atala's religion, whenever an opportunity presents itself; and remember that you promised her to be virtuous and Christian. I will watch over her tomb. Go, my son; God, your sister's soul, and the heart of your old friend, will follow you!'

"Such was the language of the man of the rock. His authority was too great, his wisdom too profound, not to be obeyed. The next morning I quitted my venerable host, who, pressing me to his heart, gave me his last counsels, his last blessing, and his last tears. I went to the grave, and was surprised at finding a little cross placed over the body, as one may sometimes perceive the mast of a vessel that has been wrecked. I judged that the hermit had been there to pray during the night. This mark of friendship and religion caused me to shed an abundance of tears. I was almost tempted to re-open the tomb, in order to gaze once more upon my well-beloved; a religious fear withheld me. I sat down upon the recently-disturbed ground. With an elbow resting upon my knees, and my head supported by my hand, I remained buried for a time in a most bitter reverie. O René! it was then that, for the first time, I made serious reflections upon the vanity of our days, and the still greater vanity of our projects. Ah! my child, who has not made such reflections? I am no longer but an old stag whitened by the winters; my years compete with those of the crow. Well, in spite of the number of days accumulated over my head, in spite of such a long experience of life, I have not yet met with a man who had not been deceived in his dreams of happiness, nor a heart that did not contain a hidden wound.

"Having thus seen the sun rise and set upon this place of grief, the next day, at the first cry of the stork, I prepared to leave the sacred sepulchre. I quitted it as the spot from which I desired to start upon a career of virtue. Three times I evoked the soul of Atala; three times the genius of the desert responded to my cries beneath the funeral arch. I afterwards saluted the East, and then I perceived, amongst the mountain paths in the distance, the friendly hermit going to the cabin of some unhappy creature. Falling upon my knees, and ardently embracing Atala's grave, I exclaimed, 'Sleep in peace in this foreign land, too unfortunate maiden! In return for your love, for your exile, and for your death, you are going to be abandoned, even by Chactas!' Then, shedding a flood of tears, I separated from Lopez's daughter, and, tearing myself from the spot, left at the foot of nature's monument a monument still more august—the humble Tomb of Virtue."

"She selected a maple with red flowers, festooned with garlands of apios, that emitted the sweetest perfumes,"

"We soon arrived at the border of the cataract, which announced itself with frightful roarings,"

EPILOGUE.

Chactas, son of Outalissi the Natchez, related this story to René the European. Fathers have repeated it to their sons; and I, a traveller to distant lands, have faithfully narrated what the Indians told me. I saw in this story the picture of the hunting people and of the laboring people; religion, the first lawgiver of men; the dangers of ignorance and religious enthusiasm opposed to the light, the charity and the veritable spirit of the Evangile; the struggles of the passions and the virtues in a simple heart; and, finally, the triumph of Christianity over the most ardent sentiment and the most terrible fear—Love and Death.

When a Seminole related this story to me, I found it very instructive and perfectly beautiful, because he narrated it with the flowery eloquence of the desert, the grace of the cabin, and a simplicity in describing grief which I am afraid I have not been able to preserve. But one thing remained for me to learn. I wished to know what had become of Father Aubry, and no one could tell me. I should never have ascertained if Providence, who guides all, had not led me to discover what I was seeking. This is how the matter came about.

I had visited the shores of the Mississippi, which formerly constituted the southern boundary of New France, and I was desirous of seeing, in the north, that other wonder of the American empire, the cataract of Niagara. I had nearly reached the falls, in the ancient country of the Agannonsioni,[12] when one morning, as I was crossing a plain, I perceived a woman seated beneath a tree, and holding a dead child upon her knees. I quietly approached the young mother, and heard her singing to this effect:—

"If thou hadst remained amongst us, dear babe, with what grace thy hand might have bent the bow! Thy arm might have tamed the furious bear, and thy steps might have outrun the flying kid on the summit of the mountain. White ermine of the rock, to go so young to the land of souls! How wilt thou manage to live there? Thy father is not there to feed thee with the produce of his chase. Thou wilt be cold, and no Spirit will give thee skins to cover thyself. Oh! I must hasten to rejoin thee, to sing songs to thee and to give thee my breast." And the young mother sang with a trembling voice, rocked the child upon her knees, wetted its lips with her maternal milk, and bestowed upon the dead all those cares which are usually given to the living.

According to the Indian custom, the woman desired to dry the body of her son upon the branches of a tree before taking it away to the tomb of its ancestors. She therefore undressed the new-born babe, and, after breathing some instants upon its mouth, uncovered its breast, and embraced the icy remains, which would certainly have been re-animated by the fire of that maternal heart, if God had not reserved to Himself the breath that imparts life.

She rose, and looked about for a tree upon which she might lay her child. She selected a maple with red flowers, festooned with garlands of apios, that emitted the sweetest perfumes. With one hand she pulled down the lowest branch, and with the other she placed the body thereon; then loosing the branch, it returned to its natural position, with the remains of innocence concealed in its ordoriforous foliage. Oh, how touching is this Indian custom! Pompous monuments of the Crassi and of the Cæsars, I have seen you in your desolated plains; but I by far prefer those aërian tombs of the savages, those mausoleums of flowers and verdure, perfumed by the bee and waved by the zephyr, wherein the nightingale builds its nest and warbles its plaintive melody. When the mortal remains are those of a young maiden suspended by the hand of a lover to the tree of death, or of a beloved child placed by a fond mother in the dwelling of the little birds, the charm is still greater. I approached her who was groaning at the foot of the maple-tree, and placed my hands upon her head as I uttered the three cries of grief. Afterwards, without speaking to the young mother, I imitated her by taking a bough and driving away the insects that were buzzing about the child's body. But I was careful not to disturb a neighboring dove. The Indian woman said to it: "Dove, if thou art not the soul of my departed son, thou art doubtless a mother seeking for something to make a nest. Take these hairs, which I shall no more wash in scented water; take them for a bed for thy little ones, and may the Great Spirit preserve them to thee!"

[12] The Iroquois,

Nevertheless, the mother wept with joy on remarking the stranger's politeness. As we were thus occupied, a young man came up and said, "Daughter of Céluta, take down our child: we will no longer sojourn in this place; we will set off at the rising of the next sun." I then said, "Brother, I wish you a blue sky, plenty of game, a beaver cloak, and hope! You are not of the desert, then?"

"No," replied the young man; "we are exiles, and we are going to seek a country." Saying that, the warrior lowered his head upon his breast, and began knocking off the heads of some flowers with the end of his bow. I saw that there were tears at the bottom of this story, so I remained silent. The mother took her son's body down from the branch of the tree, and gave it to her spouse to carry. I then said, "Will you allow me to light your fire to-night?"

"We have no cottage," replied the warrior; "but if you desire to follow us, we are going to camp on the border of the Falls."

"With pleasure," I replied; and we started off together.

We soon arrived at the border of the cataract, which announced itself with frightful roarings. It is formed by the river Niagara, which takes its rise in Lake Erie, and falls into Lake Ontario. Its perpendicular height is one hundred and forty-four feet. From Lake Erie to the Falls, the river flows with a rapid inclination; and at the leap it is less a river than a sea whose torrents crush each other in the yawning mouth of an abyss. The cataract is divided into two branches, and bends like a horse-shoe. Between the two falls there is an island, hollow underneath, and which hangs with all its trees over the chaos of the waves. The mass of the river which rushes towards the north, assumes the form of a vast cylinder, unrolling itself into a field of snow, and shining with every color in the sun; that which flows to the east descends into a fearful shade, and might be taken for a column of the water of the Deluge. A thousand rainbows bend and cross each other above the abyss. Striking against the shaken rock, the water rebounds in whirlwinds of froth that rise above the forests like smoke from a vast burning mass. Pine-trees, walnut-trees, and rocks worn into fantastic forms, ornament the scene. Eagles, carried along by the current of air, are whirled down to the bottom of the gulf; and carcajous, hanging by their flexible tails to the ends of the fallen branches, wait to seize in the abyss the crushed bodies of bears and elks.

Whilst I was contemplating this spectacle with a sort of pleasure mixed with terror, the Indian and his spouse left me. I looked for them as I ascended the river-side above the Falls, and soon discovered them in a place suited to their grief. They were lying down upon the grass, with a number of old men, near some human bones wrapped in bear-skins. Astonished at everything I had seen during the last few hours, I sat down near the young mother, and said, "What is all this, my sister?" She replied: "My brother, the earth of our country and the ashes of our forefathers follow us in our exile."

"And how," I asked, "have you been reduced to such a misfortune?" The daughter of Céluta responded, "We are the remains of the Natchez. After the massacre of our nation by the French, to avenge their compatriots, those of our brothers who escaped from the conquerors found refuge with our neighbors, the

Chikassas. We remained tranquilly with them for some time; but seven moons ago, the white men from Virginia took possession of our fields, affirming that they had been given to them by a king of Europe. So we raised our eyes to heaven, and, laden with the remains of our forefathers, started on our way across the desert. I was confined during the march, and as my milk was bad on account of my grief, it caused my child to die." As she spoke, the mother wiped her eyes with her hair. I wept also.

After a while I said, "My sister, let us adore the Great Spirit; everything happens by His command. We are all travellers; our fathers were the same; but there is a place where we shall find rest. If I were not afraid of my tongue being as indiscreet as that of a white man, I would ask of you if you have heard speak of Chactas the Natchez."

At these words the Indian woman looked at me, and asked, "Who has spoken to you of Chactas the Natchez? "I replied, "Wisdom." The Indian rejoined, "I will tell you what I know, because you drove away the flies from the body of my son, and uttered good words concerning the Great Spirit. I am the daughter of the daughter of René, the European whom Chactas had adopted. Chactas, who had received baptism, and René, my unfortunate grandfather, perished in the massacre."

"Man passes constantly from grief to grief," I replied, bending myself with humility. "You might also perhaps be able to give me news of Father Aubry?"

"He was not more fortunate than Chactas," said the Indian. "The Cherokees, who were hostile to the French, attacked his Mission. They were guided thither by the sound of a bell that was rung to succor travellers. Father Aubry could have escaped, but he would not abandon his children, and remained to encourage them to die by his example. He was burnt with great torture; but his enemies could not draw from him a single cry that might be turned to the shame of his God or to the dishonor of his country. During the punishment he never ceased to pray for his executioners, and to pity the lot of his fellow-victims. In order to compel him to betray a mark of weakness, the Cherokees led to his feet a Christian savage, whom they had horribly mutilated. But they were much surprised when they saw the young man go down upon his knees and kiss the wounds of the old hermit, who cried out to him, 'My child, we have been given as a spectacle to men and to the angels.' The Indians, furious at his expression, forced a red-hot iron down his throat to prevent him from speaking; and thereupon, no longer able to console his fellow-creatures, he expired.

"It is said that the Cherokees, accustomed though they were to see savages suffer with indifference, could not refrain from confessing that there was in Father Aubry's courage something unknown to them, and which surpassed every description of courage they had witnessed. Several of them, struck by his remarkable death, afterwards became Christians.

"From Lake Erie to the falls, the river flows with a rapid inclination,"

"On his return to the land of white men, several years later, Chactas, having heard of the misfortunes of the chief of prayer, went to gather the Father's ashes, and those of Atala. He arrived at the spot where the mission had formerly existed, but he could scarcely recognize it. The lake was overflown, and the savannah changed into a marsh; the natural bridge, which had fallen in, had buried Atala's tomb and the Groves of Death beneath its ruins. Chactas wandered about the place for a length of time: he visited the hermit's grotto, which he found full of weeds and raspberry-trees, and occupied by a fawn giving suck to her kid. He sat down upon the rock beneath which he had watched his dying Atala; but there was nothing on it beyond a few feathers fallen from the wings of some birds of passage.

"While he was weeping, the missionary's tamed serpent issued from the neighboring bushes, and came creeping to his feet. Chactas warmed in his bosom the faithful friend who had remained alone in the midst of the ruins. The son of Outalissi stated that several times, at the approach of night, he fancied he saw the shades of Atala and Father Aubry rise out of the misty twilight. These visions filled him with religious fear and a joyful sadness.

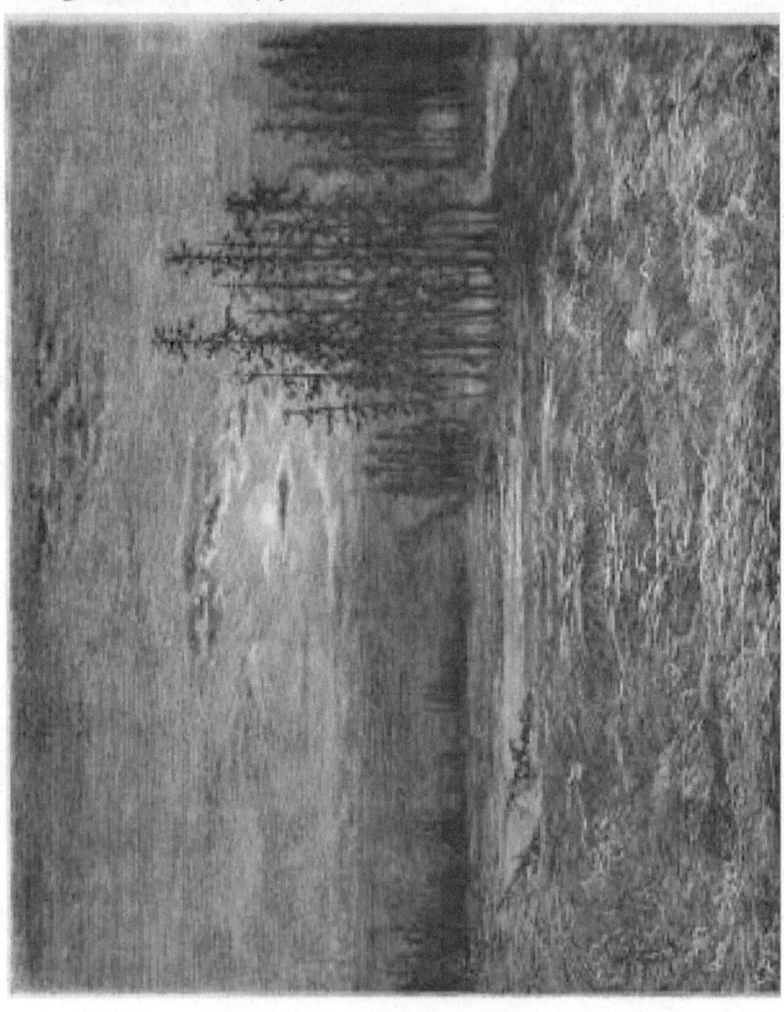

" He fancied he saw the shades of Atala and father Aubry rise out of the misty twilight,"

"After having sought the tomb of his sister and of the hermit in vain, he was on the point of abandoning the spot, when the fawn from the grotto set to leaping in front of him. She stopped at the foot of the Mission cross. That cross was then half surrounded by water; the wood of it was covered with moss, and the pelican of the wilderness loved to perch upon its worm-eaten arms. Chactas judged that the graceful fawn had led him to the tomb of his host.

"He dug below the rock that had formerly served as an altar, and there found the remains of a man and woman. He had no doubt but they were those of the priest and of the virgin, buried, perhaps, by the angels in that place; so he wrapped them in bear-skins, and started on his way back to his country, carrying off the precious remains, which sounded on his shoulders like the quiver of death. At night he placed them under his pillow, and had dreams of love and of virtue. O stranger! you may here contemplate that dust, and also the remains of Chactas himself."

As the Indian finished speaking, I rose, went towards the sacred ashes, and prostrated myself before them in silence. I afterwards walked away slowly, and with long strides, saying to myself, "Thus ends upon earth all that is good, virtuous and feeling! Man, thou art but a rapid and painful dream! Thou only existest by misfortune; and if thou art anything at all, it is merely by the sadness of thy soul and the eternal melancholy of thy thoughts!"

I was preoccupied with such reflections all night. The next morning, at day-break, my hosts left me. The young warriors opened the march, and their wives closed it. The former were charged with the holy relics, the latter carried their infants. The old men walked slowly in the middle—placed between their forefathers and their posterity, between remembrance and hope, between the lost country and the country to be found.

O what tears are shed when we thus abandon our native land!—when, from the summit of the mountain of exile, we look for the last time upon the roof beneath which we were bred, and see the hut-stream still flowing sadly through the solitary fields surrounding our birth-place!

Unfortunate Indians!—you whom I have seen wandering in the deserts of the New World with the ashes of your ancestors;—you who gave me hospitality in spite of your misery—I could not now return your generosity, for I am wandering, like you, at the mercy of men; but less fortunate than you in my exile, I have not brought with me the bones of my fathers.

Lector House believes that a society develops through a two-fold approach of continuous learning and adaptation, which is derived from the study of classic literary works spread across the historic timeline of literature records. Therefore, we aim at reviving, repairing and redeveloping all those inaccessible or damaged but historically as well as culturally important literature across subjects so that the future generations may have an opportunity to study and learn from past works to embark upon a journey of creating a better future.

This book is a result of an effort made by Lector House towards making a contribution to the preservation and repair of original ancient works which might hold historical significance to the approach of continuous learning across subjects.

HAPPY READING & LEARNING!

LECTOR HOUSE LLP
E-MAIL: lectorpublishing@gmail.com